Then he kissed her. Tender kisses in a row, leading to her jaw.

Edie tried to steady herself, tried willing herself to be calm, tried thinking of this as only a kiss—but as his lips first touched her flesh her knees nearly buckled underneath her, causing her to hold on to Rafe for dear life lest she slid to the ground at his feet. So, as her arms reached up to entwine themselves around his neck, rather than saying or doing anything that would spoil this perfect moment, Edie simply breathed out the longest, most satisfied sigh she'd ever sighed, and let the tingle of his lips trailing down the back of her neck take over.

"Maybe we should stop," she finally managed, when it was obvious he was ready to start yet another exploration. She didn't want to stop, though. Not anything. But common sense was the only barrier between her and a broken heart, and she was just coming to realize that Rafe was the first man—the only man—who could break her heart.

A new trilogy from
Dianne Drake:

With
THE DOCTOR'S REASON TO STAY
Dianne Drake welcomes you
to the first story in her
***New York Hospital Heartthrobs* trilogy**

Three gorgeous guys return home
to upstate New York. It's a place
they love to hate—until they each find a bride
amidst the bustle of a very special hospital.

THE DOCTOR'S REASON TO STAY

BY
DIANNE DRAKE

First published in Great Britain 2011
by Mills & Boon, an imprint of Harlequin (UK) Limited.
Large Print edition 2012
Harlequin (UK) Limited, Eton House,
18-24 Paradise Road, Richmond, Surrey TW9 1SR

ISBN: 978 0 263 22428 3

Harlequin (UK) policy is to use papers that are natural, renewable and recyclable products and made from wood grown in sustainable forests. The logging and manufacturing process conform to the legal environmental regulations of the country of origin.

Printed and bound in Great Britain
by CPI Antony Rowe, Chippenham, Wiltshire

Dear Reader

Welcome to **New York Hospital Heartthrobs**, a trilogy about coming home. And, I'd like to introduce you to Rafe Corbett, Jess Corbett and Rick Navarro, three real heartthrobs who have their own ideas about home. When I first learned I was going to write these books, I knew instantly that I wanted a theme about the place to which we are all connected—home. But I wanted more than that. I wanted to write stories about what compels people to want to go home and binds their hearts to that special place. In this group of stories, it was the love of a generous woman who touched countless lives…a woman much like your own mother, grandmother or aunt.

Cherished memories…that's what home is to me, and that's what home becomes for the heroes and heroines of **New York Hospital Heartthrobs**. Of course, going home isn't always the easiest thing to do. Just ask Rafe Corbett, in *The Doctor's Reason to Stay*. He hasn't been home for thirteen years, and has no intention of staying once he's attended his aunt's funeral. But it seems that a five-year-old girl named Molly, and a Child Life Specialist by the name of Edie Parker, have other plans for Rafe because, for some reason, he just can't get away, even though he's trying. Somewhere in his struggles to escape, though, Rafe finds a brand new definition of home. The question is, can he trust that home is truly where the heart is?

I hope you enjoy Rafe and Edie's discoveries in *The Doctor's Reason to Stay*. Then please, come back to see what doctor-turned-firefighter, Jess Corbett and nurse/paramedic, Julie Clark, are up to in my next **Heartthrob** story. And, as always, I love hearing from you, so please feel free to email me at Dianne@DianneDrake.com

Wishing you health & happiness!

Dianne

Now that her children have left home, **Dianne Drake** is finally finding the time to do some of the things she adores—gardening, cooking, reading, shopping for antiques. Her absolute passion in life, however, is adopting abandoned and abused animals. Right now Dianne and her husband Joel have a little menagerie of three dogs and two cats, but that's always subject to change. A former symphony orchestra member, Dianne now attends the symphony as a spectator several times a month and, when time permits, takes in an occasional football, basketball or hockey game.

Recent titles by the same author:

FROM BROODING BOSS TO ADORING DAD
THE BABY WHO STOLE THE
DOCTOR'S HEART*
CHRISTMAS MIRACLE: A FAMILY*
HIS MOTHERLESS LITTLE TWINS*
NEWBORN NEEDS A DAD*

**Mountain Village Hospital*

These titles are also available in ebook format from www.millsandboon.co.uk

CHAPTER ONE

WHOEVER said you couldn't go home again was right, in part. He was home in the physical sense now, sitting in an old wicker chair, sipping a tall glass of lemonade, with his feet propped up on the white rail separating the porch from the masses of purple and pink flowering hydrangeas traversing the front and both sides of Gracie House. Emotionally, though, Dr. Rafe Corbett was distanced from this place. Distanced by miles and year upon year of memories and pain yet so acute that more than a decade of separation felt like mere seconds. Distanced was the way he wanted to stay, however. But it was hard to do that right now, when half the population of Lilly Lake, New York, expected something of the family prodigal finally returned home.

"I see you," he said to the child sneaking up behind him. Molly Corbett, not any blood relation to him but his aunt's ward, was truly alone in the world now, and his heart did go out to her.

"Do not," she said, a little too shy for the usually outgoing girl.

"Do too," he replied. "You're wearing a red dress." Rafe flinched, thinking about Molly, then thinking about his aunt. Grace Corbett been the best person in his life, and the fact that she was gone now really hadn't sunk in. Logically, he knew she'd had a heart attack. Emotionally, he wasn't ready to deal with it. Wasn't ready to cry, or grieve, or even miss her yet, because some part of him expected her to walk through her door, tell him it was all a big mistake, maybe even a scheme to get him home to Lilly Lake. God knew, she'd tried everything she could think of these past thirteen years, to no avail.

"It's yellow, silly," she said.

"That's what I said. You're wearing a yellow dress." But, then, there was Molly, to remind him. Big, sad eyes. Clingy. His heart ached for her. She was five, and he didn't know what she understood, or didn't understand. And he, sure as hell, wasn't the one who should be trying to relate to her.

"It's not a dress," she countered, not giving over to the giggles like she normally had when Aunt Grace had brought her along on her visits.

Sighing, Rafe thought about his aunt, a larger-than-life lady who'd squeezed every last drop out of every last day the good Lord had given her. Horsewoman, humanitarian, entrepreneur, philanthropist…and what he was going to miss the most, something very simple—her chocolate-chip cookies. Once a month, come rain, shine, or any other adversity in the universe, she'd met him somewhere on neutral ground, somewhere other than Lilly Lake, and given him a tin of her cookies. Had every month for thirteen years. He'd always looked forward to it…to the cookies, but most of all to his visit with his aunt. And they'd never missed a month, until this month.

"I didn't say it was a dress. It's yellow pants."

"No, it's not," Molly said, stepping up right behind him.

"Shoes."

"No."

"Socks."

"No."

He'd been trying to draw her out the whole time he'd been here, without any luck. Oh, she'd respond when she had to. But that was all. Flat, polite responses. No emotion. Only rote words. "Hat. Purse. Hair ribbons."

"Shirt. It's a yellow shirt." Said with polite impatience. But who could blame her? She missed Aunt Grace, at least as much as he did. Maybe more, as Grace had been all the child had ever had, ever known.

Damn, he was going to miss his aunt. The ache of not having her around any more was starting to knot inside him, threatening to choke him, or double him over with grief. But Molly couldn't see that. She needed to see strength right now. All he could muster for her. All he could fake for what he was about to do…to give her away. "And that's exactly what I said. A yellow shirt. I saw you sneaking up behind me in your yellow shirt." Over the years, Aunt Grace had taken in numerous children. She'd raised them, tutored them, fostered them, cared for them, or simply given them shelter when they'd needed it—all ages, all races and nationalities. None of it had mattered when a child had been in need of a home or even a bed for a few nights. “So, Miss Molly-in-the-yellow-shirt. Are you hungry?” He asked even though he was pretty sure she was not. She’d barely eaten a thing these past few days. As her short-term, stand-in guardian, he was concerned for her well-being. As a doctor, he was worried about her health. So much grief at such a young age wasn’t good. “Can I fix you something to eat, Molly? Maybe get you an apple, or a glass of milk? Anything you want.”

She stepped around to the front of the chair and stood directly in front of him, but at a distance. She always kept her distance. She shook her head, the way she’d done every time he’d asked since he’d been here.

“Are you tired? Do you need a nap?” She hadn’t been sleeping well either.

She shook her head again.

“Are you bored? Is there something you’d like to go play with? Maybe there’s a toy you’d like for me to buy you?”

This time Molly didn’t even bother shaking her head. She simply stood there, staring at him with some kind of expectation that made him uneasy because he couldn't interpret it. Her big blue eyes were practically boring through him, telling him he should know something, or do something. But what?

That was the way it had been since he'd arrived for the funeral, four days ago, and nothing was changing except the way he felt. Molly was making him more nervous by the day. Making him feel the inadequacy he knew she was seeing. Maybe even making him feel guilty for the way he was going to have to upset her life more than it was already upset. It was something he truly hated doing, as Aunt Grace had dearly loved this child. But what he had to do was clear. He couldn't keep her, couldn't raise a child, couldn't give her the things she needed, so he'd find her someone who would.

But Rafe's heart did go out to Molly in ways he hadn't expected. She'd only lived in Aunt Grace's world, that was all she'd ever known, and now it was going to be taken away from her. She was young, though. As cute as any kid he'd ever seen. And smart. So surely some nice family looking to adopt and adore a child would be anxious to give Molly the good home she needed, the one he wanted for her. He was sure of it. Although he was also sure that being ripped from her home, the way she was going to be, would break her young heart.

That, alone, had cost him a couple nights' sleep, trying to figure out how to prevent it from happening. Problem was, there wasn't a good solution to this bad situation. He couldn't stay in Lilly Lake, and he couldn't take Molly home to live with him in his world. Neither way would work—not for Molly, not for him.

"Do you have to go to the bathroom, Molly?" he persisted, not sure what he'd do if she said yes. But much to his relief, she shook her head again.

"Look, sweetheart. You're going to have to tell me what you want. If you need me to do something for you, or get you something...*anything*...I will, but I have to know what it is." He was losing patience. Not with Molly, but with himself for not being able to connect to her. He, of all people, knew what it was like to be alone, to feel that deep-down kind of isolation. But he didn't know how to deal with it, or overcome it—not in Molly, not even in himself. On top of that, he was sure Molly wasn't totally aware of what was really going on. Maybe she had some understanding of Aunt Grace's death. Maybe she had a sense of what that meant or, perhaps, she'd guessed that it was a bad thing. But he didn't believe she truly knew that her life was about to change in big ways, ways that made him feel pretty damned guilty.

Having the proverbial rug pulled out from underneath you was never good. His own rug had been pulled out so many times he couldn't even remember most of them any more. *Or tried not to remember them.* Anyway, what he did recall was Aunt Grace always being there for him, being the one to save him and love him and protect him each and every time that rug had been yanked. The way she'd done with Molly when she'd been literally thrown away, abandoned at birth in a trash can in a bus station.

Except Molly didn't remember that, of course. What she would remember, though, was the day Aunt Grace had gone away and never come back, and changed her life for ever.

It was a sadness he shared with Molly, something they had in common. A starting place for the two of them that neither one could quite reach. It was also a terrible pain he was only now beginning to feel, one that Molly shouldn't have to deal with. But he didn't know how to protect her from it. "Does your tummy hurt?" he asked, continuing to grapple for what was bothering her.

In answer, she sighed, which made him feel even worse for not knowing. This was when he would have asked his aunt what was wrong with the child, and she would have known instantly. Except he was on his own here. Everyone had finally gone home. Summer Adair, his aunt's nurse, had returned to her old life, whatever that was. Mrs. Murdock, the housekeeper, was with her sister for a few days. His brother, Jess, had returned to his life in New York City after the funeral. Even Johnny Redmond, the man who looked after all Aunt Grace's horses, and ran her equestrian rescue charity, was keeping to the stables. Meaning it was just Molly and him now, and one of them was at a total loss.

"How about we go for ice cream? Would you like that?"

"Can I see Edie, please?" Molly finally asked.

Edie…a name he didn't recognize. "Is she one of your little playmates? Because you're welcome to invite her over. Or I could take you to her house to play, if that's OK with her parents."

No response from Molly. She simply continued standing there, staring at him, causing the tension between them to rise to the point that it was giving him a dull headache. One little girl inducing more pressure than he'd ever felt when he was in surgery. Truth be told, it was grinding him down. Besides losing sleep, he'd lost his appetite. Of course, that could also be the effect of coming home to Lilly Lake, where bad memories infused the very air he breathed. But Rafe had an idea Molly played a big part in his queasy feelings as he truly didn't relish the idea of what he had to do. So finally, in desperation, he said, "Look, Molly, why don't you run up to your room and play for a little while so I can make a phone call? After that, we'll figure out what to do with the rest of the day." Other than simply hanging around, staring at each other, not having a grasp on how to remedy the situation. "OK?"

On impulse, he held out his hand to Molly, and she grabbed hold quickly. Clung tightly as the two of them made their way through the house, now emptied of all its guests, and parted company when she continued on upstairs and he didn't. Rafe watched until Molly turned the corner, then he continued standing there until he heard the sound of her door shutting. "What am I going to do, Aunt Grace?" he asked her portrait hanging over the fireplace mantel in the parlor, on his way to the study to put out a distress call to the man most likely to know what to do. "It's a hell of a mess you've gotten me into, so the least you could do would be to tell me how I'm supposed to get myself out of it and do what's right for Molly at the same time."

Rafe actually paused for a moment, like he expected an answer from his aunt. Then, when he realized how absurd *that* was, he continued on his way, thinking about how really alone he was in this. It was him, no one else. Jess had his responsibilities elsewhere, and his own private hell to wade through every waking minute of every day. Then after Jess, there was…no one. Absolutely no one. Sure, Rafe could have easily turned and walked away, and let Aunt Grace's attorney handle the remaining affairs for him. One of those being Molly. But that wasn't the kind of person he was. He was…dutiful. That was what Aunt Grace had always said about him. Jess was sunny, Rafe was dutiful.

Except these days Jess was sad and Rafe was… well, he wasn't sure what he was. But he sure as hell was sure what he was not, which was daddy material!

The dutiful tag, though, was the thing causing the tension to quadruple in him right this very minute, as finding Molly a new family seemed almost cruel at this particular time. But she needed love, and that was something he knew nothing about. More than that, had no earthly desire to learn about. Love caused pain, and he'd had enough pain to last a lifetime. That attitude probably made him selfish, but so be it. He'd loved his aunt, he loved his brother. But no one else. It was a hard choice, but he was OK with it, for himself. Molly stood a chance at better things in this world, however, and she needed the kind of love he simply didn't have in him.

So with the resolve firmly in place that he was going to find that perfect adoptive situation for her, Rafe stepped into the study to phone the man he hoped would do most of the solving for him and shut the door behind him, grateful for the thick wooden walls that had always felt so safe to him when he was a child. All those nights when his dad had been drunk, or bellowing for the sake of bellowing, this was where he'd found his sanctuary, in Aunt Grace's study right across the street from his own private hell. In the red leather chair behind her desk, where she'd let him sit.

He ran his fingers over the back of the chair, picturing himself as a little boy, feeling so safe and important there. For a moment, when he sat down, he could almost see Aunt Grace standing across the desk from him, telling him to take a few deep breaths to help him calm down.

"Calm down," he said to himself, taking those few deep breaths, noticing, for the first time, a small, custom-made desk in the corner of the room. An exact replica of Grace's massive mahogany desk. Next to it, an exact replica of the leather chair. For Molly. The way it had been for Jess and him, and countless others.

"I don't suppose there's a simple way out of this, is there?" he asked Henry Danforth. Henry was Aunt Grace's confidant, her lawyer.

"Do you actually believe your aunt would have made things simple for you, son? She left this world the way she lived in it day after day…and you know how that was."

He did. In a word…complicated. "So tell me, what am I going to do about Molly?" Glancing at the big leather chair, then the smaller replica, he felt the first real knot of emotion constrict his throat. *I'll do my best, Aunt Grace. I promise, I'll do my best.* "And do you know where I can I can find her little playmate called Edie?"

"Shall I let him in?" Betty Richardson, Edie Parker's secretary, asked from the door separating her office from Edie's. "He's not on the appointment list, but he said he's here about Molly, so I figured you'd want to talk to him."

Rafe stepped up behind Betty, expecting to find little Edie's mother, ready to plead his case to her, but Edie, as it turned out, wasn't so little. And she wasn't anything close to the kind of friend Rafe expected Molly to have. In fact, his first impression was that Molly's friend was a very curvaceous friend indeed. Stunningly so. "You're sure that's Edie Parker?" he asked Betty, simply to make sure.

"That's Edie," she confirmed, stepping out of Rafe's way.

One without a wedding ring, he noted at first glance as he looked around the ample figure of the secretary. He also noted the long blonde hair, the blue eyes, the impeccable smile. Edie Parker, or Edith Louise Parker, as it stated on her name plaque, shoved her desk chair back and stood, staring straight at the man who hadn't waited but had followed her secretary through the office door. Yet before she could speak, Molly shot around him and ran straight into Edie's arms. "Edie," she squealed. "I was afraid I'd never get to come see you again."

Edie scooped her right in. "You know I'd have

come out to Gracie House to see you," she said, holding on to Molly for all she was worth. "I've missed you. We've all missed you."

"I don't like it there any more, Edie. It's too… quiet."

Edie glanced up briefly at Rafe. "Then we're going to have to see about you coming back to work here, at the hospital, as soon as possible. We have a lot of things for you to do. Janie, in the gift shop, needs someone to straighten her shelves. And André, in the kitchen, needs some help getting his pantry rearranged. Oh, and Dr. Rick mentioned, just yesterday, that he needs someone to help him pick out what kind of fish he's going to put into the new aquarium in the front lobby."

"I like yellow-striped fish," Molly said, almost shyly. "The ones with the blue stripes."

"Then that's something you and Dr. Rick should talk about."

For a moment, watching the exchange between Edie and Molly, the only thing that came to Rafe's mind was the phrase from an old song…something about the mother and child reunion being only a motion away… That was what it looked like he was witnessing right now, not just on Molly's part but on Edie Parker's as well. He was surprised how well they connected. Pleased, actually, as he hadn't observed that kind of emotion in Molly since he'd been here, and he'd worried about it. But witnessing Molly with Edie, he was pretty sure there was nothing to worry about. For the first time, Molly appeared a perfectly normal little girl. "I, um… Molly wanted to see you," he said to Edie, somewhat awkwardly. "Didn't mean to interrupt anything, but I didn't know what else to do for her. It's been pretty difficult these past few days."

Glancing up from her embrace, Edie answered him with a soft smile. "That's fine. I've been worried about Molly, and she's always welcome here. I'd thought about stopping by Gracie House, but I didn't want to intrude on your family at a time like this, though, so I've stayed away." She tried pushing back from Molly a bit, but the child clung ferociously. "But I am sorry for your loss, Dr. Corbett. We all loved your aunt. *Dearly.* She was a kind, caring woman. Full of compassion. She's already missed."

Yes, she'd been all that, and more. "I appreciate your sentiment, Miss Parker."

"Please, call me Edie," she said, her voice so collected and reassuring it reminded him, in a way, of his aunt's voice.

He smiled. "I appreciate your sentiment, Edie. It's been a difficult few days for everybody, and I'm not sure any of us have even begun to feel just how much she's going to be missed."

"If there's anything I can do…"

He saw sincerity in her eyes. Saw genuine affection for Molly, too, and wondered… "Maybe there is. Molly hasn't been eating well, or sleeping. I thought that spending some time with one of her playmates might help, but obviously you're not a playmate. Maybe, though, you can point me in the direction of one of her playmates."

"Actually, in a way, I am a playmate. I'm the hospital's child life specialist, which does entitle me to play with the children, along with a few other more professional-type duties." She laughed. "Although I'll admit to a real fondness for the play aspects of the job."

"Child life specialist. Isn't that a position you'd

be more inclined to find in a pediatric hospital, or a hospital with a large pediatric department?" A position about which he knew nothing at all as he kept himself locked away in the orthopedic surgery for half his practicing life, and in his office for the other half.

"Usually, but Dr. Navarro, our Chief of Staff, has plans to enlarge our pediatric ward here, and your aunt wanted me on staff before that started, to serve as an advisor for the expansion." Pushing back from Molly, she straightened up. "Oh, and in case it wasn't clear, Molly has been my *assistant* for the past three months. She's very important to the child life program we're setting up." She smiled, not at Rafe but at Molly… "An advisor."

"I have!" Molly agreed eagerly.

Rafe noted the animation in her, pleased to see it. Something about Edie Parker was causing that in Molly. Of course, as pretty as Edie was, something about her would probably cause that kind of animation in any man, including himself, fortunate enough to be around her for very long.

"When Aunt Grace comes here to work, I get to help Edie sometimes. And sometimes I get to help other people here, too, because I have lots of jobs. So, when Aunt Grace comes back, I'll come back and help again. Won't I, Edie? Just like I used to before she went away?"

Rafe and Edie exchanged troubled looks, Rafe's twisting from troubled into downright panicked. He didn't know what to say, didn't know what to do, and that must have shown quite clearly on him, as Edie jumped in for the rescue.

"Look, Molly," she said. "Right now, what I need you to do is go and help Betty. She's in the middle of a very important project, and she has a job for you." She held out her hand to Molly, and took her to the reception area, where Betty put the girl to work rearranging the boxes of toys Edie kept on hand for the kids she worked with. A very important job, in Molly's estimation. "Also, make sure nothing is broken, and if you see any toys in there that aren't clean, give them to Betty to sanitize." Edie turned to Rafe, then winked. "Molly knows how important it is to keep our toys clean."

The wink definitely caught him off guard, but so did the way Molly went right at her task, separating the toys into three boxes, one for boys, one for girls, and one for everybody, being careful to inspect each and every one. For the first time since he'd returned to Lilly Lake, he was actually seeing Molly smile. More than ever, that was a sure sign that he had no business taking care of a child. He didn't know what it took to cause her to smile, even though he'd made awkward attempts. Didn't know how to assess her needs. In fact, everything he did felt wrong. And that feeling of inadequacy was only emphasized by Molly's absence of response to his feeble attempts. The fact that even after he'd told Molly that Grace had died, her lack of understanding merely underlined his ineptness, which told him that even though he felt miserable disrupting Molly's life so much, what he had to do was the right thing.

"I figured she'd have some problems coping with my aunt's death," he said, once Edie shut her office door, "but I had no idea she didn't understand it at all. I'm sure you've already seen how much I don't know about kids."

"Don't worry about it, Doctor. Children adjust in their own way, in their own good time. Right now, Molly's just processing what's happening to her. For a child, it's difficult. But give her a little while to work through it. I'm sure she will, but if, for some reason, she doesn't, we'll try approaching it a different way, something she's better able to cope with. And that's all it's about at her age… finding that one special way that will help her cope. Because, honestly, I do think she understands. It's more a matter of her trying to figure out how to handle what she knows. That's most likely where Molly's still confused, which is why it's easier for her to ignore everything that's happened and simply return to a time when it was easier for her." She reached out, and laid a reassuring hand on his arm. "However it happens, Dr. Corbett, we'll work through it."

He glanced down at her hand, surprised by the sensation running up his arm. A tingle? "Please, call me Rafe," he said, sounding just the slightest bit unsteady.

"Rafe," she replied, gesturing him to the chair across from her desk.

He opted to stand next to the door, however. Ready to escape, maybe? Ready to throw in the towel and admit that he was totally out of his league here, and it bothered him because he was used to being the one in charge? "So, in your experience, how long does this processing take?"

Edie sat down behind her desk, folded her hands patiently and precisely in front of her, then stared up at him. "You really *don't* know a thing about children, do you?"

"It shows that much?"

She laughed. "You might as well be carrying a sign broadcasting it. Meaning I think you're going to need a lot of help. Probably more than you know."

Suddenly, the tension in him melted away. He liked Molly's friend, and he was certainly glad she wasn't a *little* playmate. In fact, he was very glad about that. "Do you like horses, Edie?" he asked impulsively, as the urge to ride hit him. He hadn't done it in years. Had put it away as part of a past he'd never wanted to revisit. Now he wanted to ride, probably the only thing that had ever made him truly happy when he'd been a kid and, more surprisingly, he didn't want to ride solitary the way he'd done more often than not back then. In fact, he could almost picture the three of them on the trail together—him, Molly, Edie. Odd, the picture of it developing. But pleasant. And totally unexpected.

"Real horses, toy horses?"

He chuckled. "Real horses. Leather saddle. A ride in the country." An idea with growing appeal.

"Horses are OK, I guess, from a distance. Why do you ask?"

"I've just decided to take Molly on a ride out to the lake later this afternoon for a picnic, and I was wondering if you'd like to come with us, maybe give me my first lesson in everything I need to know about children. Assuming that when you told me I needed help, you were also offering it."

She thought about it for a moment. Frowned, then asked, "And the horse thing…is that negotiable? The only horse I've ever ridden was a mechanical one on a carousel, and once it started going up and down, I jumped off and sat on the bench seat, the one reserved for the cowards and elderly couples who wanted to ride and reminisce."

Rafe laughed out loud, something he hadn't

done in a while. Being stuck in Lilly Lake for the next few days didn't seem as bad now as it had only a few minutes ago. Actually, he was beginning to look forward to it.

Yes, he definitely liked Molly's friend.

CHAPTER TWO

WHAT in the world had she done? Had she really accepted a date with a total stranger? Maybe even instigated it a little?

In a sense, Rafe was familiar to her. Grace had spoken about him so often she almost felt like she knew him. Well, some of him. And he was, after all, Molly's…well, she wasn't really sure what he would be called. Temporary guardian? Honorary uncle? Adopted cousin? Soon-to-be father? That was the one she hoped for. But however Rafe defined himself in that relationship, it was a difficult situation all the way round, and the day Grace Corbett had asked her to look out for Molly, she hadn't anticipated just how difficult it was going to get, or how much looking out she might be called on to do.

"I have a medical condition," Grace had said. *"Don't think I'm going to have much more time here, and I want you to promise me that you'll*

help Molly through this. I want Rafe to be her guardian and I'm going to need someone special, like you, to make sure my nephew does all the right things for her. He's got to be taught that he can take care of a child, Edie. And that he can love her. Rafe's a good man who doesn't know he has that potential in him, and I want you to guide him to that potential, to that place where he knows he can be what Molly needs, because he needs Molly as much as she's going to need him. But he's got to discover that for himself, with some gentle nudges from you."

That was why Grace had hired her, as a matter of fact. For her abilities as a child life specialist primarily, but also for those gentle nudges. Sure, the hospital pediatric department was expanding in new directions, and having a child life specialist on staff was a smart move, especially in the initial stages of the new services. But hiring her months in advance, even before the changes were to start… At first, Edie had thought it was simply good fortune, or being in the right place at the right time. But when Grace had come to her, that was when Edie had known her being there was as much about taking care of Molly as it was taking care of the children who would come to the new pediatric ward.

Funny, but in a way Grace had reminded Edie of her mother. Strong, compassionate women, both of them, always putting the needs of their children first. Edie missed her mother terribly, missed Grace, too, and, in a way, felt that maybe the two of them had connected in some karmic fashion to guide her life to this place and time, even though her mother had died years before Edie had even met Grace.

Grace had taken a big chance hiring Edie straight out of school, with no real work experience in the field except what she'd done as a student. In fact, Grace hadn't batted an eye when Edie had walked into her office that day and explained how she'd been delayed in her education, which was why she was graduating at the age of thirty-two rather than a full decade earlier, as most people in her position did. None of that had mattered to Grace. She'd hired Edie almost immediately. So now, for the unusual opportunity Edie had been given, she owed it to Grace to fulfill her most fervent wish. Yes, she'd teach, nudge, or otherwise encourage Dr. Rafe Corbett in the many ways he should care for Molly. Of course, loving that child was something Rafe was going to have to do on his own. Edie certainly couldn't force that. But Molly was easy to love. So very easy…

A knock on her office door jarred Edie's attention. "Are you busy?" Dr. Rick Navarro asked, opening the door several inches and poking his head in.

"Not really. Just trying to figure out why I got myself into a horseback ride later on, considering how horses scare me to death."

Rick chuckled. "Riding a horse is like riding a bike…only bigger, and bumpier. Horses do have a little more personality than a bicycle, though. But, trust me, once you mount up, you're going to see there's nothing else like it in the world. It's an amazing feeling, being on the back of a horse. Nothing you can duplicate with anything else. Think of it as a great big bike with legs instead of wheels, and you'll do fine."

"You have horse experience?" she asked.

"Not so much lately. But when I was a boy… my mother was housekeeper for a man who had a stable, so I got to ride just about whenever I wanted."

She could picture Rick on a horse, actually, sitting tall and rugged in the saddle. Not anything like the way she could picture herself…hunched over, shaking, holding on for dear life. "Suppose I was to tell you I've never learned how to ride a bike? That they scared me, too." As had so many things in her young life. Truth was, she'd never really had a *young* life. Most of the time it didn't matter. Sometimes, it did.

"Then I'd say you should plan on calling in sick tomorrow, because you're going to be too stiff and sore to get out of bed. And my prescription for that, by the way, will be a nice, long soak in a tub of hot water."

She really liked Rick. He was not only a great hospital administrator, he was an amazing doctor. He cared. Took time with his patients. Treated his staff with respect. Unfortunately, there were rumors floating around that he might leave now that Grace was gone and her two nephews had inherited the hospital. She was keeping her fingers crossed, though, that the rumors weren't based on fact. Lilly Hospital needed Ricardo Navarro. He brought the heart and soul to it that so many other hospitals lacked. "Well, I think maybe I'll stop by Physical Therapy later on and see if they've got any other advice for me. Or put in my reservation for one of their traction machines, since that's probably where I'll be spending the next few days...in traction."

"Cervical or back traction?" he asked, chuckling.

"Both."

"You could stay off the horse. Admire it from afar, but stay away."

Easier said than done, if she wanted to go on that picnic with Rafe and Molly, which she really wanted to do. Probably more than she was even going to admit. Her life had never really afforded her much in the way of picnics, playtime, holidays or simply relaxation, and she was looking forward to this outing. To most of it, anyway. "Or tie myself to the saddle once I'm there."

"You could also ask for a horse with short legs.

The trip to the ground isn't as far and it's less painful that way." His expression sobered. "Look, Edie, getting back to work, we're admitting a boy through Emergency right now. Keith Baldwin. He has a ruptured appendix, and he'll be going to the operating room in about thirty minutes. I need you to go down to Emergency, explain the surgery to him, make sure he understands everything that will be happening while they prep him, as well as what happens during the surgery, and especially what to expect afterward. He's awfully worried about playing baseball this summer, so talk to him about some timelines for his return, and what his recovery might entail."

It often still amazed her, all the responsibility she'd been given in this hospital. It's what Child Life Specialists did, though. They were advocates for the children, acted as the intermediaries between them and the medical staff, explained the procedures, did the reassuring, held the hands, got involved in a lot of the hugging…the best part of her job, as far as she was concerned. And she loved every second of her job. Couldn't imagine doing anything else with her life. "How old is he?"

"Eight."

"Well, luckily, I know more about baseball than I do horseback riding, so I think we'll be fine." She grabbed up her clipboard and headed to the door. Then added, "I met Rafe Corbett, by the way. He stopped by with Molly. He seems very nice."

"He's your horseback date?" Rick's words came with a scowl. A very deep scowl, in fact.

"Molly is. She's having some trouble adjusting." She noticed the frown, but it wasn't her place to ask why. She barely knew Rick and didn't know Rafe at all, and judging from Rick's reaction to the mention of Rafe, she thought it best to simply ignore the obvious friction. Still, she wondered about it, especially as both men seemed so nice, so easygoing.

Rick drew in a stiff breath then let it out slowly, deliberately, as if trying to quell something inside him. "Well, you tell Molly for me that she's welcome to come back to work any time she's up to it. We all miss her, and would love having her back at the hospital again. And I'm worried about her, Edie. As close as she and Grace were…it makes me worry about my son, and what would happen to him if…" He shook his head. "Anyway, tell Molly we all miss her."

Edie wondered about Molly's future. Maybe even worried about it. What would happen to her if Rafe *didn't* do well taking care of a child? Or, worse yet, if he turned out to be the one person in Lilly Lake who didn't love Molly?

What would happen to Molly then?

It was something Edie didn't want to think about…Molly going out to the foster-care system and being put up for adoption. She herself had endured a lifetime with that fear, living with a mother who'd had so many medical problems, a mother who often hadn't been able to care for herself, a mother who had skirted death for such a long time. At times, it had seemed like the child protective services had perched just outside the door, waiting to take Edie away to some other circumstances, waiting to put her into what they viewed as a better home.

As a child, even as a teenager, it had always scared her. She'd had nightmares about being taken away from her mother, and had spent so many fearful years peeking out the front window, making sure nobody was coming up the steps.

Sure, her life with her mother had been difficult, at times even back-breaking. But she'd loved her mother dearly and wouldn't have done anything differently. Even now, though, when she remembered all those times someone had talked about taking her away…

What they hadn't understood was that being with her mother, no matter how sick she'd been, no matter how poor they'd been, had been for the best. There'd been no neglect, no abuse. Only love. And Molly needed that now. What she didn't need, or deserve, was the awful dread that came from the knowledge that she could be ripped out of the life she knew at any moment. No child needed that. So, one way or another, Edie was determined to make sure Molly's future wasn't filled with the things she'd lived through.

Of course, her own immediate future didn't seem so bright, not when she thought about climbing up on that horse.

"She needs a good adoptive family. Actually, she *deserves* a good adoptive family. She's a sweet child and I want her to be in a normal situation. *My* situation isn't normal, there's no room for a child in it." Twenty minutes after he'd arrived home, Henry Danforth confronted Rafe, in person, with the one solution for Molly that Rafe was not going to accept. Keep her, adopt her.

"Well, then, if that's your final decision, all I can say is that we're working on it and we'll do our best. In the meantime, the county child services agency doesn't see any reason to remove her from the only home she's ever known, and stick her in foster-care. Which is what will happen if you don't look after her for now. And just so you'll know, the closest foster-mother they have is half an hour outside Lilly Lake, and she already has six children, plus three of her own. Molly would literally have to be squeezed in. So, is that what you want for her, son? To be squeezed in? Or maybe I should ask if that's what Grace would have wanted?"

He was the one being squeezed here, and Henry was so good at it. Almost as good as Aunt Grace had been. *Of course* Rafe wanted to take care of Molly in the best way possible. *Of course* he wanted her in a better situation where she wasn't going to be one of the many foster-children. "So what are you telling me, Henry?" As if he didn't already know.

"That if you want to do the *right* thing, you're either taking Molly with you when you go home to Boston, or you're staying here at Gracie House to take care of her for the time being. Which is probably what's best…letting Molly stay in her own home." He shrugged. "I mean, there aren't a lot of other good options here. I'm sorry about that, but your aunt loved that little girl something fierce, and would have adopted her if the courts hadn't said she was too old. And here's the thing. She set up a sizeable trust for Molly. You already know about that, but what I haven't told you yet is that Grace made you the permanent trustee… at least until Molly is twenty-one."

"Without telling me? Could she do that?" He was surprised yet in a way he wasn't. His aunt had always expected more of him than he expected of himself.

"Yes, she could, and that's what she did, son. You were the *only* one she wanted."

"So, let me guess. She thought I'd refuse if she'd

simply asked me, so she locked me in this way instead?"

"She *knew* you'd refuse. But Grace always got what she wanted, one way or another. Didn't mean to surprise you like I did, but that's the way Grace wanted it, too. Didn't want you having time to think about ways to back out of the arrangement."

Rafe chuckled. "I guess I should have seen it coming." He could almost see the smile on his aunt's face while she plotted this whole affair. Damn, he missed her! "So, OK. For now, that's fine. I'll serve as Molly's trustee. But I'm assuming that once she's adopted, that will change."

Henry shook his head, fighting back an obvious, devious smile. Henry was a burly man. Big, soft, with tons of gray hair on his head. And a pair of hazel, very astute eyes that missed nothing, including the fact that Grace Corbett, God rest her soul, had won this round. "The responsibility's still yours, even after she's adopted, son. Which in itself is going to be a problem, because finding placement for a child who comes with Molly's substantial financial means isn't going to be easy since there are going to be a whole lot of candidates lining up who'll want her only because she's a wealthy little girl. Of course, everything could be settled right now if you'd simply adopt her. Or at least let me write up the guardianship papers for you."

"That sounds like Aunt Grace's argument." Rafe shook his head in frustration. "But I already told you, I'd make a terrible father. And guardian. I don't have time, I don't have experience. Maybe my aunt thought that tangling me up in all these arrangements would make me want to be an instant father, but it's not happening, Henry. I care about Molly, but my focus is on my work. No serious relationships and especially no children. So it's up to you to find Molly a family who wants her because they love her, not because she's wealthy. And when you're convinced that Molly is in the absolute best situation, you can see about changing the terms of Molly's trust…phasing me out as trustee and giving the responsibility to her parents, because that's the way it should be. Or I'll have my attorney do it if you won't. Bottom line, I'm going to make sure Molly gets the best.

Personally oversee the interview process. But I'm not going to keep her."

Henry listened, still smiling and nodding as if he was *really* listening, which Rafe knew he was not. He'd known Henry since he was a child. Nice man. Devoted to the Corbett family. As easy to read as a child's picture book. In fact, Henry's *pictures* were so obvious, it wouldn't have surprised Rafe the least little bit if he'd already had Molly's adoption papers stashed away, ready to sign, with the name Rafe Samuel Corbett at the bottom. "I mean it, Henry. I'm not going to step in as Molly's father."

"I know you mean it, son. And I'm sure everything will work itself out for the best in due course. But that could take a little while. So are you willing to take care of Molly until we get it figured out?"

"Of course I will. And I'll do it right here, at Gracie House, so she won't have to be disrupted." He did have several weeks of vacation time saved up, and a host of medical partners who could take his place, so stepping out of his practice wasn't going to be a problem for a while. "But she needs her new family sooner rather than later, because I don't want her getting attached to me, then being pulled away. So work on it, Henry. Don't put it on the back burner, thinking that the slower you do this, the more I'll be inclined to keep her. That's not going to happen. And in the end Molly's going to be the one to get hurt if that's what you do." The last thing he wanted was to hurt her.

Henry nodded again, then continued like he hadn't heard a word. "I'm not going to hurt that child, son. I'll promise you that. I have only her best interests at heart." He crossed his heart. "So, let me go get started, and in the meantime I'd suggest setting up more opportunities to let Molly and Edie Parker be together. Edie's good with children. Especially good for Molly, and Grace respected that woman in a big way."

"She's not married, is she?" Rafe asked, surprised to hear the words coming from his mouth. Why did he care? Why did the image of an empty ring finger flash through his mind?

Henry wiggled his shaggy eyebrows. "Molly has good taste in friends, doesn't she? Very pretty lady. And, no, she's not married. As far as I know, not even involved. She's only been here about three months and, from what I've seen, she keeps pretty much to herself. But like I said, Grace really respected her. Took to her right away. Admired the way she worked with the children in the hospital." Henry's smile broadened. "Did I mention she's very pretty?"

"You mentioned it." And Rafe didn't disagree. Edie was pretty. Distractingly so…obviously, since that was all he had on his mind at the present.

"OK, then I'll let the child services here know you're going to stay here and take care of Molly instead of putting her in a foster-home. It's a good decision, son, one you won't regret. And you *are* doing the right thing for the child."

As Henry lumbered through the front doors at Gracie House, Rafe thought about the child who was, right now, sitting in Grace's office, trying her hardest to be a small replica of Grace. So maybe it was a good decision to stay here after all. And maybe he wouldn't regret it. But it wasn't fair to Molly. None of it was, and Molly shouldn't have to find out just how much. That was something he couldn't prevent, though. At best, he could only ease the transition because, God only knew, he didn't have anything else inside him. At least, not what Molly needed.

But Edie had it all. Everything Molly needed… It did make him wonder.

She'd spent most of the afternoon trying to avoid the obvious…her pseudo-date with Rafe Corbett. When she thought about it in terms of spending time with Molly, she felt better. But when Rafe's image entered her mind, it turned into butterflies in her stomach. He was tall, broad-shouldered. Short brown hair, dark eyes she assumed were also brown, deep tan. And a dimple in his chin. She had to admit a certain weakness for dimples, thanks to the old Cary Grant movies she used to watch with her mother on the days her mother hadn't been able to get out of bed. Butterfly-makers, for sure. And here she was, primping in front of the car's rear-view mirror, getting herself ready to go. If she had a list of her top ten most frightening things to do, riding a horse would take a solid place at number five, right after climbing a mountain, jumping out of an airplane, going to the moon and getting involved with the wrong man again.

Thinking about Alex Hastings made her shiver. Wrong man, bad marriage, regrettable decision. More than anything, a huge waste of precious time. One year in, one year out, and almost every day of it filled with regrets for the time she couldn't get back. But she'd been alone, scared, confused, and he'd been the easy port in her storm. Water under the bridge now. Regrets, yes. Huge ones, not really. Fond memories, not one.

OK, so she'd lived a sheltered life, and done dumb things because of it. She'd admit it, embrace it and, hopefully, learn from it. That was, quintessentially, her… Edie Parker, always behind, taking bad detours, slow to arrive at her life. Well, she'd finally traversed the biggest bumps and arrived. Now, no more detours. She needed to advance herself. Take graduate courses, move along even further in her career. Avoid the bumps at all cost. Or, most of them, since this little horseback excursion promised an afternoon filled with literal ones. But she was looking forward to the time with Molly. Even with Rafe. So that was the price. But the horse?

She had nothing against horses in general. In fact, she loved animals…all animals. Horses, though, only from a distance. And this seemed a good distance, sitting at the end of the driveway of Gracie House, looking well past it to the paddock full of horses, trying to convince herself she'd survive the afternoon reasonably intact.

"You accepted the invitation, so do it," she said, sucking in a nervous breath through her teeth as she turned into the drive. She drove at a pace slower than an elderly snail, all the way up to the house. Horses…Rafe Corbett…all at once? This was precisely the time when she should have been asking herself what she had done because, honestly, she didn't know.

"What the hell is she doing?" Rafe asked under his breath, watching Edie coming up the driveway, her car creeping slower than he thought a car could go.

"Looks to me like she's avoiding something," Johnny Redmond commented.

Well, Rafe knew that feeling. Aversions and avoidances. He was the master of them. Practiced them to perfection. Could write a book on all the various techniques. "Look, will you bring Donder around for me?"

"You up to that?" the stable manager asked. "He's got a lot of spirit in him, especially now that Grace hasn't taken him out for a while. Your aunt liked it, didn't want it broken down."

Rafe smiled. Donder wasn't the only one with spirit around here. Even if the spirit stepping out of the car right now was fairly tentative, it was there, as big and bold as Donder's. But with a heart equally as big. "No, I'm probably not up to it," he told Johnny. "But I want to give it a try anyway. Nothing ventured, nothing gained. My aunt subscribed to that philosophy." But Rafe wasn't sure if he meant Donder or Edie.

"Good thing you fix broken bones," Johnny said, on his way to Donder's stall.

But Rafe barely heard the words, he was so focused on Edie's approach. She was stunning. "I'm not convinced you really want to ride," he called out to her long before she was near the stable, startled by how excited he was to see her again yet not willing to admit to himself that he'd thought about her more than a time or two that afternoon.

"That makes two of us," she called back. An old-fashioned wicker picnic basket swung from her left arm, while she clasped a red plaid blanket to her chest with her right. "I wasn't sure what kind of food you were bringing, so I threw together a few things…fried chicken, fruit salad, freshly baked croissants, chocolate-chip cookies…"

"My aunt's chocolate-chip cookie recipe?" he asked, hopefully.

"My own. I had a lot of time to cook, growing up. Chocolate-chip cookies were one of my favorites to make."

Well, she had mighty big shoes to fill in the chocolate-chip cookie department, he thought. "So, you fixed all that food this afternoon?" How could anyone look so downright girl-next-door and sexy at the same time? Even the way her ponytail swished back and forth captivated him.

"I took a few hours off work this afternoon… time left over from the last holiday I didn't take.

Haven't really done much cooking for a while, and it was fun."

"Better than the peanut-butter sandwiches I was going to go slap together." Everything about her took his breath away—her blue jeans and white cotton tank top, her white athletic shoes. Simple, nice and natural. Not like the sophisticated, polished women who moved in his social circles in the city. Yet seeing Edie, he did have to admit there was a little emotion trying to creep into a place where he hadn't felt any in longer than he cared to recollect. Was it…excitement? Could he actually be a little eager over the anticipation of spending some time with her?

No, that couldn't be it. He didn't get excited. So it had to be a mild case of relief as Edie was here to stand in as the buffer between Molly and him. *Relief.* Yes, that made perfect sense. Still, seeing Edie with her hamper full of food, looking the way she did…

OK, maybe his pulse had sped up a beat or two. But, hell, he liked home-made fried chicken. Hadn't had it ages. That alone was worth a couple of extra beats. And the cookies… "Anyway, how about we find you a ride? Any kind of horse you're particularly drawn to? We've probably got just the one you want."

"Or I could walk," she ventured.

Molly stepped into the conversation at that point, went straight to Edie's side and leaned into her the way an affectionate cat leaned into a person's leg. "You could ride Ice Cream, Edie."

"Ice Cream?" both Edie and Rafe asked together.

"Aunt Grace let me name her. She was really sick when she came here to stay, and she wouldn't eat anything. But I brought her a bowl of ice cream… vanilla. And she loved it. Aunt Grace said that's what made her better again, so I thought it was a good name. And when I'm big enough to ride on my own, Aunt Grace is going to let me keep Ice Cream as my very own horse because she's so gentle."

"I think it's a perfect name for her," Edie said, slipping her arm around Molly's shoulder. "And I'd be honored to ride Ice Cream."

It was a natural gesture, Rafe noted. Not forced. Not even thought about. From where he stood, it looked like they could have, maybe should have, been mother and daughter. For a moment, he wondered if that could happen. "I think I saw her smile a little when you said her name."

"Because she still likes ice cream, silly," Molly said, giggling.

It was such a relief, seeing her act like a little girl her age should act. Rafe knew it had a lot to do with Edie, also with doing something normal from her life before all this tragedy. Unfortunately, it had nothing to do with him, for which he felt a little guilty because he felt…well, he wasn't exactly sure what it was. Left out, maybe? But that was what he really wanted, wasn't it? Not to be part of Molly's permanent situation, not to let her get too attached to him. So, in a way, he was getting exactly what he wanted, yet it didn't feel as *right* as it should have. In fact, it felt pretty darned bad, and he hadn't expected that. "Well, I think Molly has picked you the perfect horse, Edie. Care to saddle up and give her a try?"

"Me, saddle up? Sure, I'll give it a try, but first you've got to tell me which end of the saddle would face the front end of the horse?"

He chuckled. "OK, I get the hint."

"Not a hint. A blatant statement that if you want to get this picnic under way, you're going to be the one doing the saddling, while Molly and I go up to the house and make lemonade for the picnic. And I brought the lemons, just in case you didn't have any."

"I'd rather help with the saddles," Molly offered, almost shyly. "Aunt Grace let me do that sometimes, and I know how. And in case Rafey doesn't know where all the tack is kept…" She stepped away from Edie. "Do you need some help, Rafey?"

"Rafey?" Edie said, fighting back a laugh.

Molly nodded seriously. "That's his name. *Rafey.*"

A look of undiluted sheepishness, along with a fierce, red blush, crept over Rafe's face. The name *Rafey* wasn't exactly the manly image he wanted to portray to Edie, or even to Molly, for that matter. But that machismo delusion was certainly shot all to pieces now, leaving him wondering why it even mattered. Because it shouldn't. Yet it did. "That's what Aunt Grace called me when

I was a boy. She tried to stop when I was high-school age, figured it embarrassed me. Which it did. But it slipped out of her every now and again, and that's probably where Molly heard the reference."

"Uh-huh," Molly piped up. "Aunt Grace *always* called you Rafey."

"Rafey," Edie repeated, smiling. "Well, it's kind of cute, I'll have to admit. Rafey… Rafey…" she repeated a couple of times, as if trying it on for size. "Has a nice ring to it. Dr. Rafey Corbett… lacks sophistication and pretense." She grinned. "But it's good."

"Maybe it's good, but only when you're five years old," Rafe said, as the embarrassment dissolved into good nature. "Not when you're thirty-five."

"So, then, what you're telling me is that I *can't* call you…" She liked the way his discomfort gave way to ease. Rafe was trying really hard to fit in, to relate to Molly, which gave her hope. It wasn't a natural fit on him, but he was working on it and, at this point that's all Edie could ask. For now, probably all Grace would have expected.

"What I'm telling you is that you *can't*." Rafe gave his head a crisp shake in emphasis, and Edie couldn't help laughing. Rafe Corbett was a big man sitting in the saddle who was saddled with a little boy's name. It was so endearing and, for a moment, she saw some vulnerability there. A little bit of softness clouding his eyes over a nickname, perhaps? Or maybe he was only reminiscing about something nice from the time when Grace had called him Rafey. Whatever it was, it made him less stiff. Not enough to be considered loose or relaxed, but he was definitely not so starchy now. Definitely working on it, too.

"You *can* call him Rafey," Molly piped right up. "Aunt Grace did."

"*Molly* can call me Rafey," Rafe interjected. *"Only Molly."*

He said it with a little twinkle in his eyes. Or was that a challenge? Either way, it melted Edie's heart just a little bit, as Rafe clearly wasn't comfortable with the name, yet he was going to put up with it from Molly. That was just plain sweet of him. So, maybe, just maybe, her job to help him realize that he did have all kinds of father potential wouldn't be so difficult after all. She hoped so, because Rafe was a little awkward about it right now. Yet given some time, along with some good coaching…who knew? And in the future, well, who knew about that one either? Possibly, with some luck, Molly would be able to call him Daddy sooner than Edie had hoped for. That would be nice, Edie decided. What Grace would have wanted. But for a moment her heart clenched when she thought about Rafe and Molly together, just the two of them. No one else in that picture. It's what she had to do, and that was what she'd have to keep telling herself. Getting *the two* of them together was what she had to do. What she'd promised to do.

CHAPTER THREE

"COULD you two slow up a little?" Edie called from behind them. She was lagging back quite a way, not because she wanted to but because it was the best she could do. Rafe and Molly were doubling up on the lead horse, with Molly riding in a pink tandem saddle right behind Rafe, hanging on to him with her face pressed to his back. From Edie's position, it was cute. But she wondered if Rafe was bothered by it, because he looked… uncomfortable. He seemed too rigid in the saddle, even to an untrained observer such as herself. Yet Molly looked happier than Edie had seen her looking in days. Possibly because Rafe had made her happy. Or it could have been about her honest need to hold on to someone strong for a while… something Edie understood better than she cared to, given the way the first time she'd really held on to someone had turned out. Of course, everybody needed that extra jolt in their lives at some time, didn't they? Strength from someone else. Someone to support them on the journey, to guide them when they were lost.

She'd certainly had those moments in her own life…moments with her mother, moments with Alex. Good and bad. Going down the right path, going down the wrong one. Rafe wasn't the wrong path for Molly, though. He didn't know that, of course, even though Molly obviously did. Most likely, he'd never thought of himself in terms of any kind of course for Molly, which was something Edie certainly intended to change.

But the path Edie was on today had nothing to do with any of that. It was all about the path she was taking on the back of a very gentle horse named Ice Cream—a horse, as it turned out, who was absolutely perfect for a beginner to ride. Vanilla in color, she was mellow, plodding along in no hurry to get anywhere, and if it could be said that a horse was stopping along the way to smell the roses, that was what it seemed like Ice Cream was doing. Smart horse, taking in her surroundings—the path, the sky, the flowers. It wasn't a bad way to go through life, Edie supposed. Too bad more *people* couldn't take a lesson from Ice Cream. "So, when do we get to stop?" she called out, when they rounded the bend and she saw the lake ahead. "Right now, I hope, because this is a perfect place." At least, that was what her aching backside was telling her.

Like he'd been reading her mind about stopping, Rafe brought Donder, a well-muscled, brown and white Appaloosa, to a halt, then turned in his saddle to face her. "It's only another five miles," he said, without cracking a smile.

"Five?" Pulling Ice Cream up alongside him, she looked square at him and saw, up close, his very stern expression, but also saw the corner of his mouth twitch up imperceptibly in a fight to keep from smiling. "Then why don't you go on ahead, take part of the picnic food with you, while Molly and I stay here and have *our* picnic at the lake. Is that OK with you, Molly?" His eyes were dancing now. Beautiful. Mischievous. Unnerving. But she didn't look away. It took everything she had in her to stay eye to eye with him, and keep a straight face at that. She managed it, though, with some struggle. "We'll have our picnic right here, just the two of us, while Rafe goes on ahead and finds his own place to picnic."

Very straight-faced, Molly said, "You can't take the lemonade with you, Rafey. It's two against one. We get to keep it here. But you can come back and have some when you want it."

"I think you've been thoroughly told," Edie remarked.

"I think I've been charmed by the two most beautiful women in Lilly Lake," he replied, slipping down out of his saddle then lifting Molly to the ground. Heading straight to Ice Cream, he steadied the horse and held up his hand to help Edie. And in that instant, when the silky skin of her palm slid across his, if there wasn't a visible spark, there sure was an unseeable one, felt by both of them, because Edie and Rafe both pulled back in that moment of extraordinary awareness, and simply stared at each other. Speechless, almost to the point of dumbfounded. Edie wasn't sure how long it was, but the intensity couldn't be questioned. At least for her. As for Rafe…he was still holding tight to her gaze when *she* finally had to break it or become completely lost in it.

"I, um…thanks," she finally said, letting go of his hand. "For the compliment, and the help."

His answer was to arch his eyebrows. Then he turned away. Unaffected? Edie didn't know about Rafe, but she surely knew about herself, and at that moment there was nothing in her, from her head to her toes, that wasn't affected. Not one little bit of her anywhere. And try as she may, she couldn't shrug out of the mood, or even shake herself hard out of it. Not after a minute, not after five minutes. Which meant she might be in deep trouble.

"So tell me about yourself," Rafe said, as he spread the blanket on the ground. Molly was a hundred yards away, wading in water up to her ankles, looking for goldfish and bullfrogs, expressing a wish to find a whale and an octopus, too, while Edie and Rafe were laying out the picnic food. "Other than the fact that you're a child life specialist and that my aunt thought highly of you…so does Molly, by the way, that's about all I know."

"There's not much to tell. I've been in Lilly Lake for a few months now. I work, I like to read, I have a cat…" She shrugged. Getting personal wasn't easy for her because she'd spent most of her life trying to stay guarded. On purpose. One little slip of the tongue and the social workers had been on the doorstep, one misspoken word to her teacher that could be perceived as something wrong in her life and everything had gone crazy. The possibility had always been there that she could be snatched away from her mother, thrown into a foster-home where nobody loved her, and her mother forced into a nursing home until some kindly lawyer made it all better, or her mother died. Grim reality then, bad memories of it even now. "I'm from New York City originally. Born and raised there. Went to school there, didn't ever have any call to wander very far away until I took this job in Lilly Lake. And I'm not married now, but you already know that."

"Not married *now*?"

"Well, there were a couple of years in my life when I was. You know, naive schoolgirl meets big charmer. He wasn't what I needed, I wasn't what he wanted and in the end we didn't even make any memories, good, bad or otherwise. So, *you've* never been married, have you? Your aunt told me you…"

"She told you I avoid it like the plague. Right?"

"Something like that."

"Well, she was right about that. I do avoid it, maybe not so much like the plague as I do like an entanglement I just don't want to deal with. The thing is, Aunt Grace harped at me for my lifestyle, for being single. Yet she never married, and she never considered that a lack in herself."

"But she considered it a lack in you?" Edie asked.

"I don't honestly know."

"Maybe she just wanted to see you have a shot at something she missed."

He thought about that for a moment. Frowned. "She never seemed lonely, never really struck me as someone who wanted a permanent relationship in her life."

"Yet she was surrounded by so many friends, and she took in children all the time. She kept herself busy, Rafe, and she was devoted to the people in her life, but maybe, at night, when she went to bed, there were times when she would have preferred not going alone. It could be she didn't consider your lifestyle a lack so much as she didn't want you to go to bed alone every night either. I'd say that's someone who truly loved you."

"I was lucky," he said.

"More than lucky. Blessed."

Rafe was quiet for a moment, his eyes fixed on something far off that wasn't really there. Then he cleared his throat and drew in a deep breath. "So, what else is there to know about you?"

"Not much, really. I'm taking some online classes in preparation for getting my master's degree. I like gardening. Oh, and I'm thinking about getting a kitten to keep my other cat, Lucy, company, when I'm away."

Even to Edie, all the explanations sounded like uptight chatter. Nothing too significant, nothing too revealing…pretty much the way she'd trained herself to chat when people had insisted on it. It was all laid out, evenly rehearsed, rarely off the script. Reverting back to old habits was what she did when she was nervous. Rafe made her nervous.

"No family?" he asked. "Parents? Brothers or sisters?"

She shook her head. "Not any more. Maybe some distant relatives I've never met but, basically, it's just me now. And you?"

"Just Jess. And we're not really too close. We talk occasionally, see each other whenever I get to New York City…he's a firefighter there."

"I thought Grace said he was a doctor."

"He is…*was*. Trauma surgeon. But he experienced a loss in Afghanistan…his fiancée died in his arms, and he left medicine. Took up a more risky life. Don't know why, and I'm not going to argue with him about it."

"Even though you think he should go back to medicine?"

Rafe laughed. "Am I that transparent?"

"In ways."

"OK, I'll admit it. I think he should go back to medicine, but I don't really have a say in his life. And he's pretty blunt about telling me it's none of my business."

"But he's part owner of the hospital, isn't he? Along with you?"

"According to the papers. But we're not sure what we're going to do with it yet."

"Keep Rick Navarro on, I hope."

Rafe flinched at the mention of Rick's name. "Probably. I hear he's pretty good."

"Better than pretty good. He's exactly what that hospital needs, and it would be a shame to get rid of him. But I've heard rumors…"

Rafe held up his hand to stop her. "No hospital talk today. OK? Jess and I have some serious issues to address, and we're not ready yet so, in the meantime, I'd rather not get into it."

"But you'll consider my recommendation about Rick?"

"Why? Are you and Rick…?"

"No!" she snapped. "We're colleagues. That's all. Anything else wouldn't be…professional." She chanced a long look at Rafe when he glanced over at Molly playing in the lake, and what was that she saw there? Relief? Was it because she *wasn't* involved with Rick?

No, couldn't have been. Because that would have suggested something she didn't want suggested. So, like Rafe, she fixed her attention on Molly, who was thoroughly enjoying herself in the water. Too bad adults couldn't enjoy themselves that way, too. But life got in the way too often.

"I think too many people take their families for granted. You know, ignore them. Or treat them bad because they're *just* family and they know that, in the end, family will or should forgive you. Then one day they're gone—died, moved away, just drifted off—or you're so estranged from them that you might not be able to find your way back. And being alone…it's not good. Your aunt knew that, I think. But if you have family, you don't have to be alone, because being with your family is the one place you should always feel welcomed, embraced…safe."

She could hear the words just pouring out. Couldn't stop them. Didn't know where they were coming from. It was almost like she'd stepped totally outside herself to watch the delivery. "And if you have family and ignore them, or have the opportunity to have a real relationship and you don't do that…it turns into a really lonely life, Rafe. And it's not just about having someone to go to bed with, it's about having someone to sit on the porch and talk to, and call in the middle of the night when you need to hear another voice. It's about having someone who knows you so well that you don't have to say how you feel because they know. Friends, acquaintances…that's one thing. They'll stick with you, but only so far. Yet family…" She took a deep breath, forced herself to stop. "Look, I'm sorry about that. I have some strong feelings, and sometimes I just…"

Rafe chuckled. "No need to apologize. What you were saying was…was right. There's nothing wrong with having strong feelings. I've been known to have some pretty strong feelings about family myself. Just not feelings that go in the same direction as yours…unfortunately. But it doesn't matter, because I enjoyed watching you finally relax. You've been pretty tense since you got here, and it's nice seeing some of the real you getting through."

"Horses make me nervous," she confessed. "Never been on one before today, never been anywhere near one, and I've kicked myself a thousand times since I accepted your invitation because I'm usually more cautious than that."

"So, is your first experience turning out to be a

good one? If it's not, I can call someone to come get you so you don't have to ride back on Ice Cream."

He looked genuinely concerned, which touched her. "I'll be fine riding Ice Cream when we go back. She's a gentle soul, and I think she understands me." And, to be honest, she was enjoying spending time with Rafe.

"The horse? The horse understands you?"

Edie nodded. "Sure she does. As well as I understand her. She's had a lot of pain in her life, and she doesn't want to cause pain to someone else. It's pretty simple, really. Ice Cream has found her place in the world. She knows she's loved, she knows she's respected for who she is, and she's happy. Ultimately, Ice Cream has found that one place where we all want to be."

Rafe thought about that for a moment. Thought about the way Edie had connected to a simple horse. He also thought about her passion for family. She looked at life differently. Looked at it in ways he'd never considered. Gentle ways. And optimistic. Edie Parker was an extraordinary woman, and one who frightened him a little, with the way she connected to things so quickly. It was a natural ability, and one he didn't understand, coming from a life where connecting simply meant opening yourself up for more pain. Even though he was well past those days, he tried hard to be the opposite of Edie. She wanted to be connected, and flowed into it easily. Whereas he fought hard to keep his emotional distance and build up those barriers around him. He wasn't sure what to make of that.

An hour later, after they'd eaten their meal, and Molly was dozing peacefully on the blanket, curled up with Edie, who wasn't asleep but was lying there, holding Molly in her arms and simply staring up at the sky, looking as contented as he'd ever seen anyone look, he recognized that connection there again, and it rattled him to the core as it surrounded him, coming so close to touching him. OK, maybe he did envy that a little. Maybe when he'd been a boy, he might have been open to it or, perhaps, even wanted it. But that had been so long ago he didn't exactly recall all the emotional aspects of those days. Or maybe he'd just put them away, never to be brought out again.

Except, of course, Aunt Grace had been the difference, the memory that mattered. His connection. And he missed it, still needed it. Thinking back, he knew she had been his only real link to a better life, to a life where someone really did care. And now here he was, sitting on the opposite side of the blanket from Edie and Molly, totally unlinked. Totally left out. His choice, of course, and not the first time in the few hours he'd known Edie that he'd nearly regretted his choice. But even though the wounds were old, they felt more acute here, in Lilly Lake, than anyplace else. Wounds he didn't want opened again. And Edie would be the one to open them. Edie, or Molly. Not intentionally, but more as a fallout from the things he couldn't allow himself to have.

"Look, I'm going down to the lake," he whispered. "Care to come with me?"

"I'd like to, but I don't want to disturb Molly."

She connected with horses, children…probably even the ants sneaking their way up to the blanket in search of picnic crumbs. *Could be trouble,* he thought as he wandered down to the water's edge by himself. Big, *big* trouble, if he wasn't careful.

A huge part of him was on the verge of wanting to turn around and look back toward the picnic blanket, at Edie and Molly, but he knew he shouldn't. Just one look right now would change the situation from casual into something he wasn't even sure he could put into words. And he didn't like these feelings coming over him. Didn't like the mellowness, or the slender thread of longing that came along with it. Not at all!

So, he chalked it all up to this being the effect of coming home, and hoped that would take care of him until he got the hell out of there. These were old insecurities returning to haunt him, left-over emotions that apparently hadn't ever quite resolved themselves after his father had died. Damn, he hated the old man, even after a dozen years. Maybe hated him more now than ever, because those feelings his dad had burned into his soul wouldn't let go. Wouldn't even be put aside, it seemed.

After all these years being away, convincing himself he was over it, convincing himself he was well beyond the dark cloud his former life had cast over him, he despised the fact that he'd been so wrong about it, despised the fact that all the emotions had been hiding close enough to the surface that they'd simply popped out to strangle him when he let down his guard the least little bit.

But that was what was happening. Same feelings, same anger. He could feel it in his gut, feel it in his heart. And this time he didn't have his aunt to help him through it. It was just…him. No family, no friends. No one!

Unable to resist, he stole a quick glance at Edie and Molly, again seeing that easy connection between them. Even though he did envy them a little, he almost resented them for it, too. Almost resented them for something he couldn't feel. Yet, when he glanced back again, he realized it wasn't resentment he was feeling. It was…emptiness.

For a moment he caught himself wishing he could be curled up on that blanket, too, with Edie and Molly. But he knew better. If there ever was a lesson his old man had taught him, it was that he definitely could not go home. Not now, not ever. Home meant pain, and that, above everything else, was the reason Rafe spent the next half-hour standing on the shore, alone, skipping rocks.

"It's been a long time," Rafe said, extending his hand to Rick Navarro, not sure whether or not Rick would take it. To his credit, Rick took Rafe's hand right away, and greeted him with a hearty shake. But there was no sense of friendliness in his eyes. Nothing warm, nothing welcoming. Not that Rafe expected there to be. In fact, he wouldn't have been easy with it if there had been, as he didn't deserve it.

"It has been, hasn't it?" Rick said. His steady, wary gaze met Rafe's straight on. "So, welcome to Lilly Hospital… I'm assuming you and Jess are going to continue to call it Lilly Hospital."

"Actually, we haven't really talked about what we're going to do. But I don't anticipate changing the name."

Rick nodded. "Grace liked the name. She thought it sounded warm and nurturing. After she bought the hospital, the board wanted to call it after her—Grace Corbett Memorial, even Grace Memorial, but she wouldn't have it. Said it was too pretentious, that the hospital was about the town, not about her." He chuckled. "She threatened to dismiss the entire board if they went through with it. Joking, of course. But that was Grace, wasn't it? Always getting her way, one way or another."

"The hell of it was, her way was always right," Rafe said, forgetting the tension between them for a moment. "She knew it, and she had the most subtle ways of convincing other people to see it like she wanted them to. Never browbeating. Never nagging. Just..."

"Friendly persuasion," Rick offered. "She did that better than anybody I've ever known, and I respected Grace probably more than anyone I've respected in my life." He paused, drew in a deep breath. "Look, I'm sorry for your loss, Rafe. Grace meant the world to many people, including me, and we're already missing her. She always treated me fairly, when..."

Rick paused. Didn't say the rest of the words. Words Rafe knew so well in his heart. Words to which Rick Navarro had a right. "I miss her. She was one amazing lady."

That was something about which the two of

them could agree. Common ground, after all these years. "She *was* an amazing woman," he said. "And I respect her decisions about the hospital, Rick. Respect her decision to make you Chief of Staff. So let's get this awkward moment out of the way, OK? While Jess and I haven't really reached a decision over what we're going to do with the hospital, the one thing we did agree on is that we want you to stay here, in your same capacity. We don't want to make changes that will disrupt anything…not the way the hospital operates, not people's lives in general. Jess doesn't even practice medicine any more, and I have no intention of staying in town, so we're not going to interfere with anything you're doing here. Grace trusted you to run her hospital and as you're who Grace wanted, you're who I want. Can you deal with that…deal with staying on in your same capacity for now, maybe even taking on more responsibility in the future?"

Rick didn't even hesitate before he answered. "I can deal with it. But I'll need the terms laid out for me, considering…"

"Considering how badly Jess and I treated you

when we were young?" His mother had been their maid, and they'd taken every opportunity they could get to bully Rick because of it. Jess hadn't done it so much. More like stood off on the side-lines and watched. But he himself… He cringed, even thinking about what he'd done to Rick.

"You did," Rick stated. "You made my life a living hell all those years, and I know people change, but I haven't gotten over all of it, Rafe. And you've got to know it. Out of sight, out of mind works, but now that you're not out of sight, I'm having a hard time separating myself from the way you and Jess treated me. Bad memories returning to haunt me. But I'm trying to chalk it up to youthful pranks. And hoping my own son, who's six now, doesn't have such a rough time of it growing up."

"You have a son? Aunt Grace never mentioned it."

"It's a long story. Wife who sidestepped the responsibility and gave it all to me. Son caught in the crossfire. Dad with full-time custody. Christopher's a great kid. Smart, full of life. Best thing that ever happened to me. Which isn't what we're talking about here. I mean, I know what your old man did to you, Rafe. He was wrong, and I'm sorry about what he did. My mother used to tell me to be patient, that you and Jess…particularly you…weren't really such a mean boy, but looking at you through my eyes…it was tough, and there are parts of me that still resent the hell out of both you and your brother, even though I'm a man now, and I can understand where you were coming from. So you've got to know how I feel, and I'd understand if you two decided to get rid of me and hire someone else to run the hospital. This is going to be awkward for all of us, maybe for some time to come. Maybe for ever, who knows? But in my defense I can do one hell of a job for you if I stay, because I truly care for this hospital, and care for the people who work here. But like I said, you have to know how I feel about you and your brother, *personally*, before we go any further with this discussion as you may not want somebody in charge of what you own who has the kind of feelings for you that I have."

Blunt, but honest. Rafe admired that forthrightness. Respected it, even. Especially considering that Rick had a good right to his opinion. He and Jess *had* bullied Rick when they'd been kids. Kids' stuff, most of it. Unrelenting kids' stuff. But kids damaged so easily. He knew. He thought about it now, more than ever, because of Molly. Back then, he'd been a damaged kid, too, who hadn't really gotten over it yet. So he understood Rick's position. "Look, I want to apologize. Accept it or not, it's up to you. Truthfully, I don't expect you to forgive me because there was no excuse for the things I did to you." The way he couldn't or wouldn't forgive his own father. "But I am sorry for the way I treated you. It was wrong. I was wrong. And I'm not going to hide behind youthful stupidity, or give you any excuses, not even the most obvious one that I was a bully because my dad was a bully, because that doesn't cut it. Doing that would diminish my apology to you, Rick, and I don't want it diminished, because I am deeply sorry for what I did. I'm also sorry it's taken me so many years to step up and apologize." So many years to face up to the fact that he'd been just like his father. There weren't any words to describe how that made him feel, other than sick to his stomach.

"I appreciate that," Rick said, stiffly. "I do. So give me some time, OK? Let me work it out. I teach Christopher that he should accept an apology when it's offered, but doing that's harder than it sounds, I'm just now finding out. But we're good for the time being."

"Better than I expected," Rafe said. "I know that a few words aren't going to take away the impact of the way my brother and I treated you. We were wrong. Like I said, there aren't any excuses, and I don't expect that my apology is going to change much between us. But I hope I can earn your respect over time. And I do want you to know that Jess and I are aware of what you've done for the hospital and we're hoping you'll stay on."

"If I do, how will it work? How does my staying here to run the hospital really work, when you and Jess will have all the power?"

"That's just it. We don't want all the power. It's not in the best interests of the hospital. *You are.* Aunt Grace knew that, and she trusted you. Because of that, so do my brother and I, and next time he's back in Lilly Lake, he'll tell you the same thing." At least, that was what Rafe hoped. But Jess was on his own course of avoidance these days, so who knew?

Rick gave his head a skeptical shake. "Well, just so you'll know, I've already been packing up my office for the transition. I have a couple of offers I'm looking at. Nothing firm, but the possibilities are there."

"Can you unpack? Turn down the offers and stay here…hopefully for a long time. But if you can't make that commitment right now, at least long enough for all of us to figure out what we're going to do?"

"I can, but I'm a cautious man, Rafe. I have a son to think about now, and his needs come first. We've been happy here, and I want him to stay happy, but part of that is about me being happy, too. It's sort of a reciprocal relationship. So I'll have to think about it. Is that fair enough?"

"That's fair," Rafe said, pondering how the father-son relationship was a reciprocal thing. He'd never seen that in action in his own father-son situation, but there were hints of it there in

Molly. In some ways she did reflect his moods, which wasn't good as he wasn't going to be her father. "Think about it for as long as you need. And for what it's worth, you should have kicked my butt from Lilly Lake all the way over to Jasper for the way I treated you. I deserved it. Jess and I both deserved it."

Rick actually chuckled. "Is that an open invitation?"

"If that's what it takes to keep you here, it's an open invitation."

"I appreciate your honesty, and your apology," Rick said, just as his cell phone vibrated. He turned away, took the call, then turned back to Rafe, who was already half way down the hospital hall, on his way to the door. "Hey, Rafe. Care to see how we operate here?"

"As in?"

"Got an orthopedic patient coming in. A child. Probably a surgical case. I've got my surgeon on call, but if you'd like to see how things work in your own hospital, now's as good a time as any."

"Sure. Any idea what it is?"

Rick shook his head. "He fell out of a tree, so

it could be anything. I'd suggest you go get our child life specialist. The kid's only seven, and this is where Edie is worth her weight in gold."

"You're working?" Edie asked Rafe several minutes later.

"Apparently. And so are you."

She grabbed up her clipboard and headed to her office door. So efficient, he thought. He'd seen Edie in a lot of ways, but this professional look at her was new. He liked it. "He's seven, victim of a tree…or rather the ground, when he fell out of the tree."

"And he's a surgical candidate?"

"Possibly. So, how do we do this? I've never worked with a CLS before."

"It's pretty simple. You take the lead, do the exam. I follow your lead, try to figure out what kind of emotional support the child is going to need, deal with the parents, address any behavioral issues that might arise."

"In other words, you compensate for my lack."

She stopped, and turned to face him. "You lack only because that's the way you want it to be."

"We're talking about Molly now, aren't we?"

"Are we?" she countered.

"And that's supposed to be you, questioning my guilty feelings over something I've already told you isn't going to happen."

"You're right about part of that. It is your guilty feelings." With that, she turned down the hall leading to the emergency department, and shoved through the double doors before Rafe had time to articulate a comeback. Or a defense. All he could think, as he watched her disappear into the ER, was, *Wow.*

CHAPTER FOUR

"THREE ribs, one ulna, one tibia, luckily no surgery. But he's got a long recovery ahead of him." He spun away from the X-ray viewing-box to face Edie. "And since this is the third time he's fallen out of the tree, I'm going to prescribe cutting the tree down."

She laughed. "Or maybe a simpler solution, such as putting a lock on his bedroom window that he won't be able to unlatch."

"Which is why you're the CLS and I'm not."

"Trees and kids…big temptation. Bobby's just doing what any normal little boy would do when presented with such exciting temptation."

"But this temptation is going to get him killed if his parents aren't careful."

"I'll talk to them and if better locks aren't the answer, I'll bring up your idea." She smiled. "But with kids, simpler is usually the best course of action. And I have an idea that since Bobby's going to spend the next couple of months being sidelined from pretty much everything, he might not be so inclined to *escape* again."

"Ah, the optimism of a girl who probably never climbed a tree. Maybe next time we go out, I'll have to teach you to climb. Seeing the world from that high up… Definitely our next date." Pulling the X-rays off the viewing-box, he stuck them in an envelope and handed them over to the waiting ward clerk, an older woman whose scowl betrayed her obvious disdain for non-professional chitchat on the job. "Will you see that these get into the proper file, please, Wilma?" he asked the woman, reading the name on her name tag.

She cleared her throat critically, grabbed the envelope and marched from the room.

"Wilma's a stickler for professional protocol," Edie said, laughing. "And it doesn't matter if the person who's not following it *does* own the hospital."

"Then she's an asset to her job. So, about climbing that tree…"

"Never have, never will."

"Then it's not a date?" he asked, faking a sad frown.

"The only date I have is with Bobby Morrow's parents, after you talk to them about Bobby's injuries."

"Another stickler for professional protocol."

"No. Just someone who's trying to get away from the man who wants her to climb a tree. Look, you go do what you need to do with Bobby, and I'll be in there in a couple of minutes to talk to his parents. In the meantime, avoid Wilma. She'll report you to the Chief of Staff." In a flash, Edie was gone, leaving Rafe alone in the designated viewing-room, wondering why the only thing on his mind was climbing a tree with Edie.

Because he was crazy, that was why! Crazy, and borrowing trouble he didn't need.

But the image of her clinging to a tree limb, him shinnying up to rescue her… Shaking his head to rid himself of that rather nice daydream, he cleared his throat and headed back to Exam 3, chiding himself that this flirtation, even though most of it was in his mind, had to stop. Edie was

Lilly Lake, he was not. The twain that would never meet.

"So, by—" The words were barely out when Bobby's body nearly shook off the table in a huge convulsion. The first thing that came to Rafe's mind was a bone fragment broken lose and moving, or a blood clot. Instantly, Rafe pushed the emergency button on the wall near the door, then flew to the child's bed and wedged himself between Bobby and his mother, who was practically in the bed with the boy, trying to shake him into a response.

"Doctor!" she cried helplessly. "Bobby…what's wrong with him?"

"Please," Rafe said, trying to move the mother aside. But she wouldn't be moved, and when Rafe looked at Bobby's father, he seemed to be in some kind of a trance. "I need room…"

"Mrs. Morrow!" Edie called from the doorway. "Please step back from the bed."

"But my son—"

"Dr. Corbett will take care of your son, but you need to give him room."

Rafe, who was struggling to take a pulse, managed to diagnose tachycardia, meaning the boy's heart was beating too fast. "Did you give him any medication, or is there a possibility he got into something prescribed to you?" he asked the woman.

"No!" she screamed. "Nothing!"

"Nothing at all?" Rafe persisted.

"He fell out of a tree, now this…"

But what he was seeing didn't seem connected to the broken bones, and Bobby's symptoms didn't appcar to be a bone fragment or blood clot broken loose. "If he took something, I have to know what it was," he said, his patience wearing away as quickly as Bobby's life seemed to be ebbing. "Tell me, Mrs. Morrow, Mr. Morrow!" he shouted, as his patience finally snapped.

"Nothing," the woman cried. "Nothing!"

Rafe sucked in a sharp breath, then turned his back to the couple and spoke to the nurse in charge. "I need this boy treated with activated charcoal, stat. And get a crash cart in here. We also need oxygen, and get an IV in him."

Mrs. Morrow grabbed hold of Rafe's arm. "Please, you've got to help him," she begged, but he removed her hand so he could focus on the child.

"Could somebody please see that Bobby's parents are made comfortable while we take care of their son?" he barked at the crowd of people now amassed in the room—nurses, interns, lab techs, respiratory therapists…the full emergency team at the ready.

"No," Mrs. Morrow cried, as a nurse stepped forward. "I won't leave here. This is my son, you can't make me—"

"Mrs. Morrow, you must leave so Dr. Corbett can help your son!" Edie's voice was gentle but firm. Taking the woman's arm, Edie physically pulled her all the way to the hall outside the exam room, then came back and did the same with Mr. Morrow, as one of the nurses rolled the red crash cart into the area and immediately began the efforts to save Bobby's life. Oxygen, IV, heart monitor, intubation tube just in case… Rafe led the way, calling the shots, the other medical personnel responding.

About two minutes into the procedure, Rick Navarro appeared, but rather than throwing himself into the mix he took his place alongside Edie. "What happened?" he whispered.

"When I got here, Bobby was having a convulsion. Rafe was handling it, but the Morrows were getting pretty…let's just say in the way. So I got them out of the room, which is a good thing because Rafe also diagnosed tachycardia, and, well…" She glanced out into the hall at the Morrows, who were huddled together, and her heart went out to them. Too often, she'd been the one looking in the tiny window, watching the doctors frantically trying to save her mother's life. She knew what it felt like to be left out at the moment the person she loved most in the world needed her. "Look, they shouldn't be watching this, so I want to get them out of the area, unless you need me…"

"Go," Rick said. "Take them to the doctors' lounge, do what you have to."

She looked at Rafe, who caught her eye at the same time then smiled at her. He was so…in charge. Larger than life. Confident. Maybe, just maybe, she *would* like to go and climb that tree with him some time after all.

* * *

"It may have been an aspirin overdose," Edie whispered to Rafe, who was looking at the test results of blood drawn from Bobby.

They'd stabilized him for the moment. Treated the tachycardia and convulsions, splinted the broken ribs, and Rafe was in the process of getting ready to set the broken arm and leg. Overall, the kid was in bad shape, part of it caused by the fall, part of it because of what had happened afterward. "Aspirin?" he said, going straight to the result for the serum salicylate levels. Sure enough, the indication was there. "Then it's a good thing I got the charcoal into him. It was a shot in the dark, but it seemed..." He shrugged.

"Logical?" she asked.

"Kid gets hurt, he's in pain...in Bobby's case, excruciating pain due to so many injuries. And the parents' first reaction is to help ease that pain. I've seen it before. Give the child aspirin, maybe in a panic give them too much. A lot of people think that baby aspirin isn't strong enough so they load the child up and, essentially, overdose them."

"And you spotted that?"

"I suspected it. But you've got to look at a whole

list of other complications, too. Especially with children. There are so many childhood conditions that mimic something else, so you've got to be careful."

"Careful, as in suspecting it could be poisoning of some sort and treating for it before you have the lab results back?"

"Time is critical. You don't want that aspirin, or other painkiller, being absorbed into the system, because then you could be looking at a whole boatload of other complications—metabolic acidosis, renal shutdown, respiratory problems…" He shrugged. "How did you find out it was aspirin? When I asked, they wouldn't say a word."

"I told them that having the best doctor in the hospital wouldn't do Bobby a darned bit of good if that doctor didn't know what he was working with. Then Mrs. Morrow admitted giving him a couple of baby aspirin, and Mr. Morrow said it was more than a couple."

"Well, now we know what we're dealing with, so it'll be easier for us to treat Bobby. Thanks for getting it out of them because I sure as hell didn't have the silver tongue to do it."

"Maybe because you were too busy saving Bobby's life."

"Or maybe I lack the people skills."

"Aren't you being a little too hard on yourself?" Edie asked.

"What I'm being is honest. Nothing else intended. I treat conditions of the bone, it's what I do, it's who I am. The rest of it doesn't matter." With that, Rafe spun away and returned to the treatment room, ready to finish the process with Bobby Morrow and his parents. It wasn't his intention to be rude to Edie, or to even shut her off, but he didn't like compliments, didn't like anyone glowing over his work. He did what he did, and that was all there was to it. Oh, he liked being an orthopedic surgeon. Actually, he loved it. But he didn't want, didn't need accolades, and as sure as a new day rolled around every twenty-four hours, Edie had been on the verge of accolades. So it had been easier to leave. But he felt a little rotten about it. She'd done a masterful job of getting the information out of Bobby's parents. It probably wouldn't have hurt him to lay a few accolades on her. Hindsight, he thought, as he walked through the door to Bobby Morrow's treatment room. It was a kick in the rear end. Too bad he hadn't used a little foresight.

"I come bearing a peace offering," Rafe said, setting the cup of hot tea down on Edie's desk.

She looked up at him. "For what?"

"I was pretty rude to you earlier. Didn't mean to be, but that's how it happens with me sometimes. It just slips out."

She hadn't taken it personally, though. He'd been a little abrupt, but not so much that she'd been offended. "A real apology would have included a vanilla bean scone with the tea," she said, pulling the cardboard cup over to her, "but I appreciate the thought."

Rafe laughed. "You're a tough one, Edie Parker."

"No one's ever accused me of being tough before. I think I like it."

"Look, sometimes I get…preoccupied with my work, and…"

"And you don't take compliments very well."

"That, too."

"Well, how about a hand signal? Maybe a subtle

salute, or a half-wave? That way, it's not a real compliment, but you'll know one was intended."

"Tough, and relentless. Not a bad combination, actually."

"No one's ever called me relentless either. Normally I was the gushy one, the one given to the biggest emotions, the one who sort of got shoved to the wall when the room filled up and I didn't know how to fight my way to another spot. But I appreciate the description. I aspire to being tough and relentless."

"Would you aspire to grilled cheese sandwiches and tomato soup from a can tonight? I promised Molly her favorite meal, figuring I'd be ordering take-out pizza or something, and that's what she wanted. So I'm going to be donning my chef's apron and whipping up a culinary masterpiece later on, if you'd care to join us."

She laughed. "A man who cooks? How could I refuse?"

"Actually, I have ulterior motives. I'm pretty sure I can handle opening the soup cans, but grilling the actual sandwiches may be well beyond my culinary capabilities."

"What do you do back in Boston?"

"Eat at the hospital cafeteria, or order in."

Edie shook her head. "Bet you don't do your own laundry either."

"As a matter of fact…no." The way her eyes twinkled when she laughed caught him off guard. He really didn't intend to stare, but he couldn't help himself. She had such depth. More than that, she had a spirit like he'd never seen in anyone before, and he was pulled in by it. Edie was a woman who generally cared about everybody. She couldn't help herself. It's what she was about. And, honestly, other than his aunt, he'd never known people like that existed. "But I do bundle it up and haul it down to the laundry myself. Even sort it."

"A man who sorts laundry and opens cans of soup…"

She gave him a salute, *and* a half-wave. But the thing that caught his heart most was her smile. He was already addicted to it, and even though that should have worried him in a big way, it didn't. The fact that he wasn't worried didn't worry him either. Actually, he spent the rest of the day enjoying the lingering results of something as simple as Edie's smile.

* * *

"And for dessert, I have a surprise," Rafe said, setting the silver-domed platter on the picnic table on the patio. Soup and sandwiches had gone down well and Edie and Molly had done all the preparations while he'd stood back and watched them interact. It had occurred to him, more than once, that Edie would be the perfect parent for Molly. Their genuine affection for each other showed, and they had a natural rhythm together, one that would cause anyone looking on to see them as mother and daughter. That, plus the fact that they simply looked the part.

Could it work out? It was a thought, maybe even a good one. And somewhere, in the back of his mind, he'd even considered that if he did manage to make it happen, he might be able to keep himself on the fringes of the relationship. Seeing Edie again…he wouldn't mind that. Wouldn't mind having some insignificant part in Molly's life either. "And I'll have you know that I spent all afternoon in the kitchen…" He whisked the lid off the dome. "Arranging these vanilla bean scones on the platter."

"What are they?" Molly questioned.

"The perfect accompaniment to hot tea," Rafe answered.

Molly wrinkled her nose. "But we're not having hot tea."

"No, but Edie did earlier today, and the person serving her the tea neglected to get her the scones so he's trying to do a make-good."

"And succeeding very admirably," Edie commented. She turned to Molly. "When I was a little girl, there was a tea room a few blocks from my house."

"What's a tea room?" Molly asked.

"It's like a restaurant, only every afternoon they serve tea and little sandwiches or scones. You get all dressed up to go there because it's a very special place, and once a month my mother and I would put on our best clothes, catch the bus, and go to the tea room. She liked the little sandwiches with her tea…they had fillings of cream cheese and cucumber."

"Yuck," Molly said.

Edie laughed. "My opinion, too. I loved the scones. Sometimes they were lemon, sometimes butter toffee. Always delicious. So, now, when I have tea, I like to have a scone with it."

"Do you and your mother still get dressed up and go to the tea room?" Molly asked.

"No. My mother went…well, she went to the place Aunt Grace is now."

"So you have to have your tea and scones all alone?" Molly's face was deadly serious when she asked the question. "Because I'll come with you, Edie, so you don't have to go by yourself. But I don't want those yucky sandwiches. I think I'll have the scones, too."

Rafe shut his eyes, shut out the emotion of the moment. Dear God, his aunt had done such a good job with Molly. It touched him, the way it had just touched Edie, who was brushing tears from her eyes. He knew what he had to do. The only thing was how was he going to do it? More than that, how was he going to do it and *not* get involved himself?

"Not good enough," Rafe told Henry Danforth. "The Simpsons seemed too preoccupied with image, the Walcotts weren't concerned enough with a proper education, and I don't know how you slipped the Bensons on the list because the only reason they wanted a child was to have an indentured servant."

"You've turned down seven perfectly good families, Rafe," Henry said, his irritation clearly showing. "I pre-interviewed each and every one of them myself, had my investigator do an exhaustive background check, and I can assure you these are all good families for Molly."

"But not good enough!"

"So who is it you really want? Because I'm sensing an agenda."

"My agenda is doing the best thing for Molly. And who I really want…?" He hadn't said it aloud. Hadn't even let himself think it in a couple of days because if he had, and Edie wasn't agreeable, he wasn't sure what he'd do. She was the perfect mother for Molly. In his mind, the only perfect mother. The thing was, she hadn't said a word about wanting to adopt Molly. Sure, Edie's agenda was to get him to keep her. Aunt Grace wouldn't have manipulated it any other way. But Edie knew that wasn't going to happen. He'd made himself perfectly clear. So, to be honest, he was a little disappointed that Edie wasn't stepping up because from everything he'd seen between her and Molly, she should have been.

Of course, from his detached perch, maybe he wasn't seeing this the right way. It was a distinct possibility, but one he didn't want to admit. Not yet, anyway. "Who I really want is the person who wants Molly the most. But she…or he…has to also be the person Molly most wants."

"Which wouldn't be you," Henry snapped.

Actually, that didn't sound so good to him any more. It was still his reality, though. Maybe a more bitter one than he'd expected. "Which wouldn't be me."

"Fine. Let me go and break the hearts of all the people I've interviewed so far, then start over."

"I'm not wrong here, Henry. None of these people have been right for Molly."

"And if they're not right for her, and you're not right, who is?"

"Edie Parker," Rafe finally confessed.

"Edie?" That seemed to catch the old lawyer off guard. "Have you talked to her about it?"

"No, because she's involved in this and she knows Molly is—"

"Up for grabs?" Henry interrupted.

"She's not up for grabs!" Rafe huffed an impatient breath. "And you know that!"

"What I know is that you're ignoring the obvious and if your aunt were here, God rest her soul, she'd be drumming, kicking or pounding some sense into you right this very minute."

But good sense didn't involve adopting a child who needed so much more than a man who didn't have it in him to love that child the way she needed to be loved…the way he'd never been loved. When it got right down to the most cutting truth, he *was* his father's son. He'd read to the end of the book. He knew how *that* story turned out. He wanted better for Molly. "If my aunt were here, she'd be the person Molly needs most. But since that's not going to happen, we have to do our best to find the person who has all the qualities to replace my aunt. Those are some mighty big shoes to fill but, for Molly's sake, we've got to fill them." And Edie was the only one. But what would happen if he asked, and she turned him down?

"Then I'll ask Edie."

Rafe shook his head. "No. She needs to ask us. Edie needs to be the one who realizes she wants Molly without us asking her." For the sake of two people who really did belong together, he firmly believed that.

"In the meantime, should I line up more interviews?"

On one hand, if Edie did say no, then they'd be back at square one, which meant he'd have to prolong his stay in Lilly Lake to reopen the search. That part didn't matter so much, but Molly's emotions did, and that was what had him worried. She needed to start her new life…her real life…now. Without delay. Yet he couldn't even think in terms of someone other than Edie raising her. "No more interviews for now," he finally said.

"Then you've changed your mind, and you're going to ask Edie?"

Rafe shook his head. "Edie's going to ask me."

"You're that sure of it?"

Truth was, he wasn't sure at all. But he hoped, like he'd never hoped for anything else in his life.

"I'm not sure of anything, Henry. Not one damned thing, except that Molly needs to be with Edie."

Henry cocked a bushy eyebrow then exited the den, smiling. And whistling.

"I'm *not* going to be the one to keep Molly," Rafe shouted after him. To which Henry did not reply.

"It's not as easy as it looks," Edie said, looking at Rafe in the mirror. "First, you divide her hair into three sections, then your job is to alternately cross each outer section, one at a time, over the center section. And make sure it's consistent." She was demonstrating braid technique on her own hair for him. "I mean, you're a surgeon, you've got good hand technique, so how hard should this be?" He was cute, actually. All thumbs and frowns. She liked the vulnerability she saw in Rafe when it came to Molly. He tried so hard to please her, which gave Edie hope that Rafe might be reconsidering his position.

"Let's just say that by the time I got through with her, she was in tears. This party tonight is important to her, and she's set on having her hair braided."

"Then I'd say that if you're not up to it, take her to one of the salons in town. While you're at it, does Molly have a new dress to wear?"

"She has a closet full of clothes."

"But a new dress for the party?" He was such a man! She didn't mean that in a bad way, but Rafe was so…oblivious. Definitely oblivious to little girls, probably to women as well. "And shoes! She has to have new shoes to go with her new dress." With a couple of twists, her hair turned into a perfect braid, and she spun around, smiling at him. "See, not that difficult."

"Then maybe you could braid her hair tonight. And take her shopping for a new dress and shoes."

"Or maybe you could," Edie suggested. Sure, it would have been easy enough to do that for Molly, and having a girls' afternoon out would have been fun. But that was something Rafe needed to be doing. He was the one who had to get closer to Molly, who had to see how much fun she would be in his life. He was also the one who had to discover, for himself, that Molly was the person he most needed to fill out his life. In other words, open himself up to her. She could see the signs, see Rafe's willingness to do anything he thought was necessary for Molly, see how he tried hard to be responsive. But she also saw the way he kept himself distanced. It was like he was going through the motions yet not letting himself fully invest in them. An hour in a beauty salon could help that. Watching Molly try on ten or twenty pairs of shoes definitely would.

"With a woman's touch?" he asked. "Would you come with us? I'll do what needs to be done, but if this party is so important to Molly, I think you being there to help in her decisions would be a good idea. Especially as this is the first time she's really ventured out since…"

Well, Rafe had her on that one. Maybe Molly did need the extra emotional support. God knew, she'd needed it after her mother had died. Needed it in ways she hadn't seen coming. In fact, she'd needed it so desperately she'd pretty much jumped straight into a bad marriage on her first time out, and while Molly certainly wasn't at risk of that, Edie did understand the emotions involved in moving on. "I'll go, as long as you're not backing out of this."

"Not backing out," he said, on an obvious sigh of relief.

"Oh, and just so you'll know, we should pick out the dress first so Molly can have co-ordinating hair ribbons. Things like that are very important to the total ensemble." Was that panic creeping to his face? Actually, it looked adorable there, and she really wanted to laugh at his discomfort over such simple little-girl things, but she wouldn't. Rafe was trying hard to do the right thing for Molly, even though he was that proverbial fish out of water. "It's going to be fun. Just relax. Enjoy yourself."

"Fun? Back home, I have a shopper. She's a nice lady who has a thriving business going, shopping for people like me who find it easier to pick up a phone and tell her what I need rather than going out buying it for myself. And I have a barber who makes house calls. These people do what they do for me, first, because they're making a good living at it and, second, because for me, shopping and going to the barber shop *isn't* fun. It doesn't make me relax, and I never enjoy myself doing either!"

"Well, it *could* be fun, if you were doing those things with the right person." Did he ever allow himself to relax? Even in something as simple as shopping, Rafe kept himself distanced. In a way, it was sad he limited himself the way he did. It almost seemed like he was afraid to let himself go even a little.

"Well, *you're* the right person for Molly. I want to make this fun for *her*."

"But not for you?"

"What I want for me is to make sure Molly gets what she needs to make her happy. That'll be sufficient for now."

It wasn't exactly what she'd wanted to hear from him, but somewhere in his words lurked a pure motive. It was better than nothing. "Then I say let's go down to the stables, get Molly, and see what kind of power shopping we can get ourselves into."

"Power shopping?" Rafe actually moaned aloud. "I thought this was about a dress, a pair of shoes and a perfect braid."

Laughing, Edie whisked around him and headed to the door. "It's never just about a dress, a pair of shoes and a perfect braid."

Prophetic words, as it turned out. Because three hours later, with no less than five dresses, six pairs of shoes, and more accessories than Edie could count, and a pair of cowboy boots Molly just had to have, the three of them stumbled into the beauty salon ready for the next part of the adventure. Or, as Rafe would put it, ordeal.

"She'd like…" Rafe started to tell the beautician, but Edie laid a hand on his arm to stop him.

"She can do that," she whispered to him. "Part of this needs to be a teaching experience, too."

"Maybe you should make me a list, telling me everything I should know, because I'd have never guessed that a hair appointment could also be turned into a teaching experience."

He dropped the shopping bags on the floor then slid into one of the chairs lined up along the wall. It was pink, rather undersized for him. He looked awkward, but cute, she thought. In the past three hours, her estimation of Rafe had grown about a hundred times more. He was patient, considerate…not very adept at little-girl things but trying harder than anybody she'd ever seen. "With kids, everything can turn into a teaching experience. The thing is, they don't have to know that's what it is. Right now, Molly's involved in a huge decision that's going to affect the outcome of her evening. All those books the beautician is taking to her… they're full of different hairstyles suitable for a child her age. Molly's going to get to choose."

"But I thought she wanted a braid. Isn't that pretty simple?"

Edie laughed. "I'm afraid you've just wandered into a very complicated world, Rafe. There's nothing simple about a braid. I'm mean, there are so many types… French braids are one of the classically most popular. It's where hair is woven in small chunks on top of the main braid, which lies close to the scalp. The final result is a tidy and very sophisticated look. Maybe a little too old for Molly, but who knows? Then there are herringbone braids, which are thin, layered braids that use a number of small intertwined pieces of hair. And lace braids, which are simple braids that crown the head of the wearer in a half-moon shape, like a tiara. Personally, I think that would be a lovely choice for Molly. But she might like cornrows or Dutch braids, or…"

Laughing, Rafe held out his hand to stop her. "OK, so when you said there was some teaching value here, I didn't know I was the one being taught. So, a braid is not a braid is not a braid."

"You're catching on."

"Just like a party dress is not a party dress is not a party dress."

"Has it been that awful for you?"

"Not awful so much as…exhausting. She tried on that pink dress three times then bought the blue one instead."

"And she might still change her mind and want to exchange the blue one for the pink one. That's a woman's prerogative."

"My world's a whole lot simpler. You just—"

"I know. Call your shopper, and wear what she picks out. But where's the fun in that? I mean, think about it, Rafe. What would happen if you took Molly out shopping for you? You might discover that there's more to life than gray dress slacks and blue dress shirts."

"How do you know that's what I wear?"

"You're predictable. Sure, you're in jeans right now. But you're out of your element. What happens when you get back into your element...your rut?"

"I wear gray and blue, which suit me just fine, thank you very much!" He said this almost defensively.

"But what if Molly found you a pink shirt or, heaven forbid, navy-blue slacks? Could you handle that?"

"It's just colors. What's the big deal?"

"The rut's the big deal." She didn't know if he liked his rut, or if it was just easier for him being stuck in it.

"So, when is a shopping trip *not* a shopping trip?" he asked. "When it's meant to show me just how much I need to be a father?"

"I'm not denying it," Edie said.

"And I'm not buying into it," Rafe argued.

But he was, hook, line and sinker. She knew it. And an hour later, when Molly hopped out of the beauty chair, her hair done in a pretty lace braid, the look Edie saw on Rafe's face only confirmed how much he was truly buying into everything.

"She's beautiful," he whispered, his voice full of emotion. The emotion a father would have for his daughter.

It was such a touching scene, it brought tears to Edie's eyes, and she turned her head quickly so Rafe wouldn't see.

"Rafey," Molly called out. "Can we take the blue dress back and get the pink one?"

Rafe laughed out loud. "Of course we can." He gave Edie a gentle nudge, then held out his hand for Molly. "I wouldn't have it any other way."

CHAPTER FIVE

IT WASN'T like she was a schoolgirl out on her first date yet somehow that was exactly how she felt. A little bit giddy, a little bit nervous…all of it probably owing to the fact that she hadn't actually been out on a *real* date with Rafe yet. Or, for that matter, any kind of date for some years. Occasionally, there'd been casual coffee at the corner coffee house or lunch with a casual friend… Casual, casual, casual…that was about as far as her life had gone in the dating department since her one and only venture into the real relationship world had sent her running for shelter before the ink had barely dried on the marriage certificate. She took the blame…all of it. She hadn't been ready to be out in the world on her own let alone tied into a relationship. But marriage had seemed stable, and she had been at a place in her life where she'd wanted stability. Alex, though, he'd wanted a real marriage…something she hadn't been able to give him even after the hasty vows had been pronounced at the county courthouse. Oh, she'd playacted for a while, fashioned herself in the role and given it her best effort, but her best hadn't been good enough. So after that, no men, no dates until now.

The thing was, Edie wasn't even sure that this qualified as a date. As they were exchanging Molly's blue dress for the pink one, a mention of dinner had slipped into the conversation, barely without noticing. Then the next thing she knew, she was home worrying, primping and worrying some more. Admittedly, she was attracted to him. What woman wouldn't be? Big, rugged, handsome. The kind of man who brought a sigh to her lips…lips she'd tried to keep *those* kinds of sighs away from for a long time. After all, what was the point? She'd dipped her toe into that pool once and found she didn't like getting wet. So why bother with the sighs when she wasn't willing to allow anything more?

Except with Rafe those sighs seemed inevitable now, even when she fought them off.

Well, she'd just have to deal with it, wouldn't

she? Keep her distance, as well as a good, hard bite down on her lower lip. “Besides, it’s just a silly little dinner,” she chided herself, looking at her reflection in the mirror. “Food, conversation. A way for Rafe to kill a couple of hours waiting for Molly to be finished at her party.”

But who was she kidding? She *was* nervous. No avoiding it. Suppose they got on too well, or discovered they didn’t get on at all? How would either way affect her quest to win him over to adopt Molly? What she did, or said, could have such a strong bearing on Rafe’s intentions with Molly, and that was the thought that pestered her for the next ten minutes, until the doorbell rang.

“Rafe, it’s so nice to see you,” she said, trying not to sound breathless when she opened the door to him. Her first look at him nearly took her breath away, though. Casual jeans, tight. Boots. Close-fitting T-shirt showing off a nice expanse of chest. Leather jacket. Everything about him impeccable. Not bad at all, she decided as he helped her into her wrap. Actually, very good…his look, her reaction. Because she was still focused on her mission in spite of Rafe’s incredible good looks. This was about Molly, not about her. So, it was all under control, she decided as Rafe took her arm and led her down the walkway to his car then helped her in. *About Molly*, she kept telling herself the whole way to Mama Bella's World Famous Pizza.

"You don't mind casual tonight, do you?" he asked, holding open the restaurant door for her. The hostess, a jovial, matronly woman with short red braids who spoke with a fake Italian accent, showed them to a secluded table for two, probably the table considered to be the restaurant's most romantic, even though the tablecloth was red-and-white-checked vinyl.

"Excuse me?" she asked, biting back a smile as he was pulled out the chair for her.

"Casual. You don't mind making this a casual evening, do you?"

"But doesn't the candle on the table automatically make it romantic? Most of the other tables don't have candles." The candle was a drippy red thing, burnt down to a stub, stuffed into a used wine bottle.

In one swoop Rafe grabbed up the candle and put it on the floor. "There. Casual."

In a way, that was disappointing, not that she'd expected a romantic evening with him. Or even wanted one. But to dismiss it so quickly…to just whisk the candle off the table the way he had, was, oddly, a letdown she hadn't expected. *It's about Molly,* she reminded herself. "There, casual…" she said, picking the candle up off the floor and handing it to a passing waiter. No more hints, no more reminders, no more awkwardness…at least, on her part. "OK?"

"Well, it occurred to me that I should have mentioned what I had in mind for this evening, so you could dress appropriately."

"I'm not?" she asked, suddenly self-conscious. She was wearing black slacks, a simple powder-blue sweater, something that should have covered both worlds—casual or dressy. Even romantic. Damn, did he actually think that was what she thought? Now she felt awkward again.

"And I've gone and said the wrong thing, haven't I?"

"It shows?" she asked.

He smiled. "You don't hide yourself very well,

you know. Everything shows on you. But it's nice. Very nice."

"So what you're saying is that I wear my heart on my sleeve?" This wasn't the first time someone had told her that. In fact, that was what her mother had always said.

"And a very nice heart, and sleeve, they are. Oh, and before I put my foot back into my mouth, let me just say that you look beautiful this evening. That's what I was trying to say a minute ago when I went so horribly wrong."

"Not *horribly* wrong. Just a little wrong. And you're forgiven."

He laughed out loud. "Beautiful and brutally honest. No wonder my aunt liked you." Settling in, Rafe stretched back in his chair. "Look, Edie, let *me* be brutally honest here for a minute. I don't...don't date. Don't do relationships."

"And you think that's what my accepting your invitation is about? That I'd want a relationship... with *you*?" She could already feel the flush rising in her cheeks. "That I'd accept a date for pizza and expect a side order of commitment to go with it?"

Immediately, Rafe went rigid in his chair. "I feel my foot wedging in my mouth again."

"Both feet," she snapped. Sure, she was angry. And humiliated. Embarrassed, too. So much so that she tried to shove back her chair so she could stand and muster the dignity to march out of there. But Rafe stood first, caught her by the wrist on her way up, and had the decency to look a little embarrassed himself.

"Could we just start this over?" he asked.

"There's nothing to start over," she said, not sure whether she wanted to sit back down or stand all the way up and leave, the way she'd planned.

"I was trying to explain myself, Edie. That's all. Trying to tell you a little bit about the way I am… which, as you can see, is pretty damned pathetic."

Admittedly, he did look pathetic. Which was why she sat back down. She *was* curious about Rafe, was interested in hearing what made him tick. "OK, tell me. But it had better be good, Rafe Corbett, because so far I'm not impressed with your dating manners."

"Neither am I." He let go, then sat back down. "Which is why I need to explain myself. The thing is, Edie, I really don't date, don't get involved. For a lot of reasons I don't want to get into this evening, it's easier that way. So I'm rusty."

So this *was* a real date in spite of what he'd said! Not a romantic date, but a date nonetheless. Suddenly, she was nervous again. "Trust me, you don't know rusty. That's my middle name. But, in my defense, it's fine. I don't date, per se, either. Bad marriage aside, dating's scary."

"Ah, yes, the marriage thing. You don't seem like the type who would un-commit once you've committed."

"Well, I'm probably not, under normal circumstances. But it was a low point in my life. I was desperate, afraid of being alone, he seemed…nice. And he was. But not for me. So my mistake cost me a lot of time, but I suppose you could say I came out of it wiser."

"Let me guess. You're older and wiser, and you've taken some kind of vow against marriage. You're never going near it again."

Edie laughed. "Well, maybe I won't go quite that far. But I did take a vow that the next one has to be the right one. The one and only. And my list of qualifications going in is pretty long, and stringent."

"You have a list?"

"That's the only way to do it these days. You decide what you want, and—"

"And go shopping with your list." A fake frown covered his face. One that gave way to an amused grin. "I think you're on to something, Edie. Maybe I should make a list of my own."

"Starting with?" she asked.

"Hands down, this is the list topper. She has to make me laugh. Everything else is negotiable."

"Then you're pretty easy to please. Some lucky lady's going to find you irresistible just for that alone."

"*That* alone?" He faked a wince. "That cuts to the core of my ego. A man likes to live in this delusion that he's irresistible in *other* ways. You know, that list thing. Most men do have their lists."

And Rafe's was a very long list. In fact, there was practically nothing about him that wasn't irresistible. Which was turning into a big problem. "Well, in the defense of some men, maybe it's not a delusion. Of course, maybe the list isn't as long as they think it is either. But I suppose irresistible is in the eye of the beholder, isn't it? And depending on the beholder, that list could be very long, or very short. So, if your only real requirement is that she has to make you laugh… " Edie leaned across the table to him. "I won't say this too loud since you apparently don't want to get caught, but you could be a sitting duck if you want to be. Look around you, Dr. Corbett. The world is full of women just waiting for the snap of a finger."

He leaned even closer to Edie. "The thing is, Miss Parker, I'm probably the hardest man to please you'll ever meet because I don't laugh."

She pulled back then folded her arms across her chest. "But you do, Rafe. All the time. Especially around Molly."

"So to *you* that means that Molly is the one who's supposed to catch me?"

"So to me that means you don't know yourself as well as you think you do."

"And *you* know me better than I know myself?"

Edie didn't answer that. She didn't have to, because the answer was obvious. At least, to her it was. In this matter, she *did* know him better. Which meant her biggest task was to introduce Rafe Corbett to Rafe Corbett. Unfortunately, that was easier said than done. More than that, she wasn't sure how yet.

The next fifteen minutes passed in a nondescript blur of inconsequential small talk—weather, current events, hospital—over a frosty pitcher of beer and, finally, a pizza. "Aunt Grace used to bring me here," he said, as the server made a tableside production of cutting the pizza into slices. "Lilly Lake's done a lot of growing since I've been gone, but this place…nice memories. Not much change either. Especially here," he said, taking Edie's plate and holding it up for the first slice.

"It is nice," she agreed. Nice ambiance, the smell of the pizzas was wonderful, the servers all friendly…she felt good here. Felt like she belonged, which was something she hadn't felt since her mother… "We used to have a little deli down the street. It was a lot like this place. Not fancy, but nice. You felt welcome, and sometimes, when my mother was feeling up to it…" She smiled, fighting back the memory. They hadn't been able to afford the deli, but Mr. Rabinowicz, the owner, had never turned them away.

"You mother was sick?"

This wasn't the topic of conversation she'd hoped for over dinner, but she'd started it, after all. "Sometimes…most of the time. But we managed…" She smiled sadly. "Most of the time."

"Care to talk about it?"

"There's not a lot to say, really." She stared down at the slice of pizza on her plate. Didn't want to see his expression, didn't want to see his sympathy, or pity, as the case may be. She'd seen that too often in her life, didn't want any more of it. "My mother had pernicious anemia. It was diagnosed when I was seven and lasted until, well…" She didn't have to say the words. He was a doctor. He knew the consequences of a condition where, in even the best cases, survival was measured in remissions and relapses that never stretched out into a normal life span. "Mum had good days as well as bad ones in the early years then we hit a mid-point where the doctors thought she might be achieving some sort of remission. False hope, of course. But it was nice while it lasted. Then came the relapse, and as the disease progressed to its end stage, the bad days started outweighing the good ones. That's the nature of the disease, as you know, and the more debilitated my mother became, the more I took care of her. Consequently, I had more responsibility at home than most girls my age did." Finally, she gained the courage to look at his face, and what she saw there was so compassionate it brought tears to her eyes. He wasn't pitying her, or looking at her as some kind of martyr. He was simply understanding her words, maybe even understanding a little bit of her heart. Which scared her in ways she didn't understand, in ways she didn't want to understand.

"And you wouldn't trade those years for anything, would you?" he asked.

"No, I wouldn't. My mother was this wonderful fount of so much knowledge and love, and I never saw her frown, never even saw her get angry. I mean, she went through the worst, things you can't even imagine, and she did it with so much grace and strength. She had a tough life, raising me alone, not much money coming in, always up and down in her health, but she never complained, never felt sorry for herself."

"No father?"

Edie shook her head. "He left before I was born. Didn't want the responsibility. The only thing my mother ever said about him was that he didn't have the heart for it."

"Kind words for a man who didn't deserve them." Rafe said, not even trying to hide the bitterness in his voice.

"Maybe he didn't, maybe he did. I'll never know, because he was killed when I was a toddler. My mother always said that he was a sad man who didn't know how to follow his heart, and that's how I like to think of him…as a sad man. And the thing is, even though I never met him, what I learned from him is that people don't follow their hearts the way they should. They get so caught up in what society expects or dictates, or whatever other trappings are out there ready to grab them, they forget to follow their hearts. But every day my mother showed me how much that mattered, showed me how to do just that, no matter what else was going on."

"She sounds like she was an amazing woman," he said, as sadness washed down over his face. "I'm sorry she's gone now. Sorry I'll never have the chance to know her."

"She *was* amazing, and I'm sorry about the way *your* father treated you. Grace told me some of it, and there are rumors…it was horrible, Rafe. You deserved better. But you had your aunt…" She reached across the table and took hold of his hand. "Grace found me when I was pretty lost, you know. Sheltered life, failed marriage, fresh out of college a decade later than I should have been and totally without a clue, and there she was, a great big miracle in a tiny, feisty package, crooking her finger at me, telling me to follow her." She paused, swiped at a stray tear that had found its way down her cheek. "I'm glad I did, because what I have found in Lilly Lake is…everything." Her path finally restored. "I'm happy here, and I'm sorry you can't be."

"It's that obvious?"

She shook her head. "Grace warned me."

He chuckled. "It seems my aunt was the prognosticator of a great many things."

"And a good judge of pizza," she said, picking up her slice, glad for the opportunity to change the subject. She held it out to touch it to his slice in a toast. "To Grace Corbett," she said. "A woman of influence and perfect insight."

"To Grace Corbett" he said, smiling fondly. "A woman who knew her heart."

"She did, didn't she?" Edie asked.

He nodded. "Not only did she know her heart, she knew everybody else's." With that he took a bite of the pizza.

Edie filled up after one huge slice, and Rafe went on to eat three before he was feeling the need to loosen his belt. One last swallow, and one final sip of beer swigged, and he pushed his plate and beer mug away, then settled back in the chair. "So, what's next?" he asked Edie.

"As in?"

"As in, are you planning on staying here? Settling down, making Lilly Lake your permanent home?" It was occurring to him that if he succeeded in persuading Edie to adopt Molly, it might be good to give her Gracie House, so Molly wouldn't have to be uprooted.

"Maybe. I haven't really thought about it in the long term. In the short term, I love my job, I'm renting a nice little cottage…it's good. I don't really have a reason to go anywhere else."

"But if better job opportunities came up?"

She frowned, clearly puzzled by this line of questioning. "What's this about?"

"Just curious. I mean, I do own the hospital, so I have a vested interest in what you do since…"

"Since I work for you? Have you turned into my employer now?" Said in quite an irritated voice.

"True, I own the hospital. That's all paperwork and legalities, nothing to do with the actual operating of it. But I was just curious about you. Future plans, hopes, dreams…"

She eyed him suspiciously. "Future plans—keep on working. Hopes—keep on working. Dreams—get an advanced degree and keep on working. Is that what you wanted?"

OK, he was doing it again. Opening mouth, inserting foot. He hadn't meant to. In fact, he'd hoped to settle back into a nice, relaxing conversation and approach the subject of Molly's future. But he'd put her on edge…*again*. Which meant any talk about Molly wasn't going to be met with the most receptive attitude. "What I wanted was to start a nice after-dinner conversation with a lovely lady. But the lady seems to be taking it the wrong way."

"Or the gentleman seems to be starting it the wrong way. Look, Rafe, I like you, but this…this so-called date isn't really a good idea. We did better when our mouths were full, but now that we have to actually sit back and talk to each other…"

"And you wonder why I don't date," he huffed.

"It's not you. It's both of us. I have my agenda, you have yours…"

"What if our agendas overlapped?" he asked. "Would that be common enough ground to keep us on this date for another few minutes? Because, as bad as I am at it, I don't want it ending so soon, Edie."

"Why?" she asked, trying to mask all emotion in her face.

But he saw the emotion…the warmth in her eyes, the way the corners of her mouth turned up ever so gently. She couldn't help but care, couldn't help but put herself out there for someone who needed her. And while he wasn't about to admit that he needed her, he would freely admit that Molly did, and that was what this conversation had to get on to. Molly. "Because I like being with you," he said, kicking himself for those misspoken words before they were all the way out. He should have told her it was about Molly. Had meant to tell her it was about Molly. Then he'd gone and said he liked being with her. Another kick to the head. "And I have a bad habit of shutting out the things I really like. Over the years, I've developed this uncanny way of letting in only what I want to let in, and shutting the rest of it out. It keeps things in good balance that way, and my old habits aren't yielding very much this evening, for which I truly am sorry, Edie."

"There's no need to apologize for you being you. But what I have to wonder is what happens if you shut something out that really would have been nice to let in?"

"Do you mean Molly?" he asked.

"That's not where I was going with this, but we could turn this into a conversation about Molly, if that's what you want to do."

"Maybe we should, because Molly's my priority, over everything else, and I'm counting on you to help me with her. The thing is, I'm not shutting her out. I'm opening new doors for her. Or trying to." Trying hard to open Edie's door and, so far, failing miserably.

"Opening her doors, shutting your own at the same time. Isn't that what you're doing, Rafe? Because I wonder what would happen if you could keep *all* the doors open for a little while…yours and hers. Give it some time, see what happens, instead of being so…so stubborn about it. You know, forget the open doors for now and try being open-minded for once."

He arched amused eyebrows. If there was only one thing he could say for Edie, it was that she was fierce in her loyalties. Of course, he was glad he didn't have to say only one thing because that list she'd mentioned earlier, the one with her stringent qualifications…well, he had a list, too. And it all concerned Edie. But nothing on it was stringent. More like, it was a list of attributes… lovely to look at, nice to talk to, wonderful to just sit back and watch… "Did you know you fairly glow when you're impassioned?"

"And *you're* condescending when I'm impassioned. This is a serious discussion, Rafe. Don't deflect it by telling me I glow."

"OK, so maybe I'm deflecting. I'll admit it. Talking about Molly's future is difficult. But, Edie, you've got to understand, I don't have many doors in my life, open, shut, or otherwise. I'm all about structure. I live by it. I'll die by it. Everything in my life is so damned structured it's like I stay on a very linear, very narrow path, and I can't get off it. But I don't want to get off it because it works for me. Me. Alone. Nobody else involved. I accomplish what I want to, have everything I need, and the thing is, I *do* want what's best for Molly, which is *not* my life. I wish it could be, because that would be the easiest thing to do. I genuinely care for that little girl. But she needs more than I can give her, more than I can be for her." More than his own father had ever been for his sons.

"And you can't adjust your life just a little to

accommodate her? I mean, how do you know that if you haven't tried?"

"I know it because…hell, it's complicated." He shifted in his seat. "Look. I am who I am, and while I may not be the person you want me to be, I have the good sense to know my limitations. Getting involved with someone else in a way that matters…that's my limitation. It's not an excuse. It's a fact."

"But what if there's something else inside you, Rafe? Something you're not seeing, or something you're trying hard not to let get through?"

"Yeah, the Rafe Corbett who's just waiting to be some poor little girl's daddy. Well, that's not me. And if that's what you're seeing, you'd better look again." He huffed out an impatient sigh. "Look, I'm sorry. I wanted this to be a nice evening, but with Molly's situation hanging between us… I feel horrible about what I've got to do, Edie, and you're seeing the fallout from that."

"Then the simple solution is not to do it."

"Easy to say, impossible to do. Sometimes we don't get what we want, no matter how hard we try to make it work. That's just a fact of life, like it or not." Tonight he didn't like it one little bit, because he could almost see himself staying in Lilly Lake, settling down, raising Molly, maybe even he and Edie… No! He blinked it out of his head.

"But sometimes we do get what we want. It might be a struggle, or it might be a battle like we've never fought. My mother always told me that if there was something out there I wanted badly enough, I'd find a way to have it. And I believed her. I mean, look at me. Who knew I'd ever get this life? I started late, messed myself up before I hardly got started, yet I'm here. And before you go and tell me something like what I wanted was simple, and what you want isn't, don't. I never had simple in my life. Not for one minute. What I had, though, was desire, and that's what got me through."

"And I'm happy for you, Edie. I know it wasn't easy, and I know your dream wasn't simple. But you had a dream. That was a starting point."

"And you don't?"

"What I have is a function. I like being an orthopedic surgeon. I'm good at it. I take great satisfaction in helping people. But is it a dream? Or have I ever had a dream?" He shook his head, trying to remember a time when he'd had a dream. And came up blank. Well, almost blank. Because for the first time in his life he was feeling some regrets. Which meant there must have been some kind of a dream in there somewhere. As further proof, when he looked over at Edie, his heart clenched. So he blinked away from her in an instant and set about the task of blinking away what had just happened to him.

"But why can't you embrace what you have and, at the same time, try for more? You're a talented doctor, but can't you define yourself some other way? Something that isn't about your function but about your...your heart?"

"My heart? It beats, Edie. It's a biological necessity to keep it beating if I wish to continue living. Which I do. But the rest of it...the romantic notion that my heart can dictate something in my life? I don't buy into it. Which is precisely why I can't be Molly's father. She needs someone who subscribes to the whole theory that the heart is more than an organ in the body. And don't go looking all sad on me now that you know you're not going to win this argument, and get Aunt Grace's way."

"My way, too, Rafe. Molly is meant to be with you. When I was younger, I chose to go one way. Then when I got a little older, I made another choice. We can make those choices in our lives, but we have to take the first step, which is admitting we want that change. So why limit yourself, or even stop yourself where you are, if you want more? And I think, deep down, you do. Otherwise you wouldn't be so torn up about finding a family for Molly."

He didn't have an argument for that. No comeback, no response. Edie was right, of course. But how could someone who was so full of love understand someone who was not? In her rose-colored world, love took care of everything. In his world, love didn't exist. It was easier that way. It didn't open him up to be hurt. And he was better at being alone than anybody he knew. So why change it, and take the risk?

And why bring someone else, like Molly, or even Edie, into his misery, if he took that risk, and failed? *You're just like your father, Rafe*. Just like his father. How many times had he heard that throughout his life, and how the hell could he wish that on anyone? "Care for another beer?" he asked Edie, more with the intent of grappling for conversation to clear his head of the dark thoughts rambling around in there rather than offering an actual beer, which he was pretty sure she would refuse as she'd hardly touched her first one.

"One's my limit," she said, pushing away her still half-filled mug. "I'm full. Good pizza, good beer, interesting conversation..."

So, this was it? The end of the evening? A little conversation, a little food, then what? Rafe wasn't even sure this warranted a circumspect kiss at the front door when he dropped her off. Which, in the end, turned out not to matter, as Henry Danforth called before they made it to the car, telling Rafe that he'd brought Molly home from her party, and she seemed a touch under the weather.

"Probably nothing," Rafe said as they headed out the door. "Kids pick up bugs all the time." Yet only two hours ago, all decked out in her frilly pink dress, she'd seemed fine. No symptoms, no nothing. Just a normal child with an exciting evening ahead of her.

"Want me to come with you?" Edie asked. "I know you're the doctor, but she might need…"

"Mothering?" A chance to see how much Molly needed Edie.

"A woman's touch. And if you could see the look on your face right now…"

He bent down, took a look in the rear-view mirror, saw the worry mixed with stress, tried pretending it didn't exist. "Looks normal to me," he lied.

"Looks nervous."

He chuckled. "OK, so maybe I'm a little overanxious. But I've never had a kid to care for, and I don't really know much about them."

She climbed into the car, and Rafe shut the door behind her then went round to the driver's side. "Good parenting is a lot about good instincts. Don't over-think it, Rafe. It's all really pretty simple. Give her the basics—food, shelter, clothes, education, add love and support and some wise guidance along the way, and she'll turn out to be amazing."

Maybe so, but not for him. "Guaranteed?"

Edie laughed, then reached over to squeeze his arm. "With Molly, yes. Guaranteed."

His inclination was to kiss her now, before the evening turned crazy. But she fell back into her seat too quickly for that to happen, fastened the seat belt almost instantly, and pretty well sent out some very strong body language…all of it negative. Naturally, he didn't blame her. He hadn't handled this evening well. Thank God, Edie was good-natured about it, because any other woman would have left him before the beer arrived. But Edie…she was different. The more he got to know her, the stronger his conviction became that she would be perfect…for Molly.

For some lucky man, too. Edie and another man…a thought he shoved right out of his head.

"I think she's feverish," Henry Danforth explained. He had almost leapt out the front door to greet them, he was so anxious over Molly's condition. "I thought about taking her straight to the hospital, but seeing you're a doctor…"

Rafe laid his hand on the man's shoulder to reassure him. "You did the right thing. I'll go take a look, and if she needs something I can't do for her, I'll get her admitted in a few minutes. But most times these things turn out to be nothing."

"I was worried I might have done something wrong. When I got the phone call…by the way, her little friend's mother called me because Molly said you were on an important date tonight and couldn't be disturbed. Anyway, Grace always told me I was like a bull in the china shop when it came to children, but I never took her seriously. And when I got the call, I wasn't sure what to do. Maybe I should have…"

Rafe silenced him with a squeeze, gently nudging him toward the door. "I'll call you later. Go home, relax. And don't worry about it, Henry. You did the right thing, bringing her home, putting her to bed, and calling me."

"She's a little flushed, Rafe," Henry said on his way out the door.

"And I'm sure she'll be better in the morning."

"Well, call me, one way or another. You know how I care about that child."

Everybody did. Which made Rafe feel guilty,

as he was the lone hold-out, the one who couldn't care enough. "I'll call. Now, go home, go to bed."

As it was to turn out, his "next morning" prognosis was a little off. Molly had a good case of flu. The two days in bed type, Rafe feared, once he had a look at her.

"And now we're exposed," he said to Edie, who was already placing cold compresses on Molly's forehead. "Sorry about that."

She laughed. "I work with children, get exposed to things every day. I've got pretty good immunity built up. Haven't caught a thing from anyone yet. In fact, one of the reasons I chose to work with children is that I seem to have a high level of immunity, at least from the common, everyday ailments like colds and flu. Kids are living, breathing, breeding grounds for bacteria and viruses, and my stamina has come in handy. So, do you want me to spend the night?"

An offer he wanted to accept in a different way, one having nothing to do with taking care of a sick child, but, having her here to take care of Molly would have been nice. But having her here would have also been too cozy, and he was beginning to think of Edie in terms of someone *other* than the woman he wanted to be Molly's mother. Those feelings, in fact, were springing on him much faster and stronger than he could have ever expected. Not good.

Rafe reached out and took her hand, pressed a set of car keys in them. "I appreciate the offer, but we're good. How hard can it be, taking care of a sick kid? Keep her hydrated, keep her rested..."

Edie laughed. "Bet you won't be saying that tomorrow. When kids are sick, they have this way of getting really—"

"Annoying?" he asked, smiling.

"More like rambunctious, needy, lots of whining. Their energetic little bodies aren't meant to be sidelined, and while the wise doctor in you will know that Molly needs more rest for a full recovery, Molly's going to be telling you, and showing you, the very opposite. So, call me when you're overwhelmed, because I have a few sickbed tricks up my sleeves." She held up the car keys. "Thanks for the ride. I'll bring it back tomorrow."

"No hurry. I have an idea I won't be going anywhere for a couple of days."

"Then maybe I'll stop by with a care package after work. Are you *sure* you can take care of her by yourself?"

"Guess we'll find out, won't we?" He walked with her to the front door then opened it. "Look, Edie. I'd like to do this again before I leave Lilly Lake. Another night, no flu. Maybe something other than pizza. Do you think we can manage that?"

Another date? He was actually asking her out on another date? She was sure they could manage it, but with the way her pulse was racing, she wasn't sure she should. "Let's wait until we see what this strain of flu holds in store for us, OK?"

He chuckled. "Well, I've got to give you credit for one thing. That's the most original turn-down I've ever received."

"Not a turn-down, Rafe. I'd really like to go out with you again. And for two people who basically don't date, or get involved with anyone else, that's a pretty big step. But you're not going to be here much longer, and with Molly's needs to see to, I'm not sure that the two of us getting together is really a priority. Plus, I'm betting you'll probably be sick with flu in a couple of days. So…"

"So it's a maybe?"

"*Possible* maybe."

"And if I don't start showing any flu symptoms in a couple of days?"

"Then I'll upgrade the prognosis to a probable maybe." She stood on tiptoe and kissed him on the cheek. "I had a nice time this evening, Rafe. Thank you."

He frowned for a moment then shrugged. "As I don't know if we're going to get to do this again, I might as well go for it."

"What?" she asked.

But he didn't answer. Instead he pulled her into his arms and lowered his face to hers. "Incubation time for most common viruses is one to three days so I could already be infectious. There's still time to back out."

"But I've got good immunity," she said, tilting her head back as all willpower flew right out of her. "Great immunity, and…" And she wanted this. Didn't kid herself that it could be a one and only, because for them that was most likely their destiny. But she wanted this almost as much as he did, and she was ready to take the step that crossed the line of no return. Knowing what she did, that nothing could or ever would come of this, the prudent choice would have been to step back, but there was nothing prudent in her as she pressed herself hard against his body. "Just this once," she whispered, staring up into his eyes. "Because we know who we are."

But looking led to touching and more senseless ideas than she could deal with. His hands splayed on her spine, working their way down from her shoulders to the hollow curve at the small of her back. His body, hard with an arousal she couldn't explore, crushed unrestrained to hers. Her attraction level was crazily out of control now. Sure, she'd admit it. She was attracted to Rafe in ways she hadn't known attraction could exist. The other aspects of his life, of her life, though…the ones that were invading her mind…that was the real problem. Except at this moment she wouldn't allow the problems to beat them.

"You're sure?" he asked, his voice so low she barely heard it.

She nodded, tried to speak, but there were no words as Rafe pushed her hair aside, pulled down the neckline of her sweater, but only enough expose the skin over the tender place where her neck and shoulders met. Then he kissed her there. Tender kisses in a row, leading to her jaw.

Edie tried to steady herself, tried willing herself to be calm, tried thinking of this as only a kiss, but as his lips first touched her flesh, her knees nearly buckled underneath her, causing her to hold on to Rafe for dear life, lest she slide to the ground at his feet. As her arms reached up to entwine themselves around his neck, rather than saying or doing anything that would spoil this perfect moment, Edie simply breathed out the longest, most satisfied sigh she'd ever sighed, and let the tingle of his lips trailing down the back of her neck take over.

"Maybe we should stop," she finally managed, when it was obvious he was ready to start yet another exploration. She didn't want to stop, though. Not anything. But common sense was the only barrier between her and a broken heart and she was just coming to realize that Rafe was the first man, the only man, who could break her heart.

Suddenly, all the need in her turned into trepidation.

"You're not enjoying this?" Taking over with his fingers, Rafe kneaded her shoulders then started down her back.

Enjoying it? She was enjoying it more than he would ever know. "It's not..." His hands skimmed over her ribs and came to rest in the small of her back, eliciting an involuntary moan from her. "Not right." Breathless words. "We're not supposed to be..."

"Not supposed to be what?" he whispered in her ear as he placed a kiss there.

It would be so easy to get lost in this, to forget that he didn't ever commit, that she wasn't ready to commit again, but... "Mmm..." she mumbled, as his hands descended ever so slightly lower, nearly, but not quite to the round of her bottom. Her eyes flew open as the pressure of his slight squeeze jolted her out of the moment. "Rafe, we can't." She tried forcing conviction into her voice, but she couldn't do it. It simply wasn't there to be found.

"Fine, if that's what you really want..." As he spoke the words, though, his hands continued their journey, not down but to her hips. Which was where he stopped. Which was where he pulled her so roughly into him that there was no question what came next. Not now, not in the next hour or two.

"It isn't," she forced out. "What I want is..." she whispered, "is one moment."

Rafe cupped her chin in his hand and tilted her face up to his. "Only one moment?"

Edie swallowed hard as his gaze fell to her mouth. She could feel his heat, feel the sparks arcing back and forth between them, feel everything... "Maybe two or..."

Before the rest of her words were spoken, Rafe lowered his lips to her. Kissed her hard at first. Kissed her out of pure frustration and raw want. But the kiss melted into tenderness as his tongue slid back and forth across hers. His mastery of such a simple thing sucked the air from her lungs and caused her to forget that they were standing on the front porch of his aunt's mansion, caused her to forget that this was only a moment and there might never be another one. In that time, there was *only* that moment, *only* that tangle of emotions she so desperately feared.

Her kiss to him came on a moan as she pressed herself even harder against him and snaked her left leg around his right. Rafe groaned with pleasure, a heady sound she enjoyed almost as much as she enjoyed the taste of him—the tantalizing reminiscence of pizza and beer. Shamelessly, she ground herself into him, found his erection, and nuzzled it into her belly, then rocked back and forth into him, into his arousal. Then she gave herself to his hand pressing underneath her sweater, seeking out her breast…the ache of pure, sexual desire cresting in her in a way she'd never before felt. And would never feel again.

Reality, in all its ugly manifestations, came crashing down. They couldn't do this. Nothing about them was about…*them*. Except that one new feeling she had. And she truly didn't know what to do with it, or about it. So, she stepped back, took a firm hold of his car keys, and prayed her legs would take her all the way down the walk to the car.

When she got there, after she'd managed to get the door open, she finally allowed herself a look back, to see if anything about Rafe looked the way she was feeling. But he was gone. The porch light was still on, and the front porch was totally, completely empty.

CHAPTER SIX

"RAFE, I need your help." Rick Navarro's voice came over the cell phone.

He'd barely had time to check on Molly. So far, she was sound asleep. Resting pretty comfortably, actually. Now he was sitting in a chair, staring out the window at the night sky, hoping for sunrise, hoping for a new day to begin, seeing that he'd gone and messed the old one in ways he didn't even want to think about.

It could have been a simple kiss, should have been a simple kiss… Hell, who was he kidding? He'd wanted Edie like he'd never wanted another woman in his life. Hence the topic of his current thoughts. *Why had he wanted Edie like that?* He wasn't kidding himself about the answer. It was about a lot more than just the physical urges. A whole lot more.

The thing was, he wasn't finding an answer. Or maybe he didn't want to find one. But now it didn't matter. Rick was on the phone, saying something about needing him.

"I can't come. Molly's sick," Rafe said.

"That's what Edie just told me. So I've got Summer Adair on her way over to look after Molly. She was your aunt's nurse."

He'd talked to Edie? How was Edie sounding? he wondered. Just as confused as he was? "What's the emergency?"

"Accident. We have casualties…multiple car pile-up out on Route 9. Roberts Turn. Small van full of children involved."

Children involved. Suddenly everything else in his mind was pushed aside. "Any other information?"

"Not yet. I'm on my way to the scene. We've got firefighters on the way, and I've called some extra staff into the hospital. Don't know what to expect, though. Reports from the scene are pretty spotty."

"OK, I'll be there as soon as your nurse shows up. I'm probably twenty minutes out once I hit the road." Without a car! Or ten minutes by horse. As soon as Rick hung up, he called the stable and asked Johnny to saddle Donder. The way it turned out, Johnny was ready to ride with Rafe by the time he reached the stable.

"Just keeping track of the horses," the older man said.

"Or keeping track of me," Rafe said, climbing up into the saddle.

"I'm not saying that you're out of practice or anything, but it's been a while since you've had a good hard ride, and I just want to make sure nobody gets hurt."

Rafe smiled. "Me or the horses?"

"Your aunt did love her horses, son. But as far as I could tell, she loved you, too. Don't expect she'd have wanted either you, or her horses, getting hurt none."

Taking the reins, Rafe turned Donder toward the stable doors, wondering how often doctors made house calls on horseback these days. In a way, he liked it. "Giddyup," he said, nudging the stallion in the side.

Donder whinnied, snorted in a deep breath, then Rafe was off. Black horse, black night. Somehow he felt exhilarated, felt more alive than he had since…since he couldn't remember when.

Too bad it was Lilly Lake doing this to him, he thought, turning just short of the pine grove beyond Gracie House and heading down the trail leading to the back door of Roberts Turn. Too bad, because he liked the way he felt. Could almost imagine himself living here, doing something like this more often.

But it was Lilly Lake. And that was always the bottom line.

"Seven children, five adults involved," Rick shouted in greeting as Rafe climbed off Donder and handed the reins over to Johnny. "We've assessed a couple of specific orthopedic injuries. Stabilized them for the time being, but we may need to send you back to the OR to take care of them if we can't get hold of Dr. Wallace."

"Who's Wallace?" Rafe asked, practically running alongside Rick.

"Our orthopedic surgeon. We share him with the clinic in Jasper, as well as the hospital in Beaver Dam and the one in Redbird."

"I didn't realize that resources were stretched so thin here."

"Well, doctors don't really want the small-town life so much these days. So you have to make do. We're pretty good at it."

That was not what he wanted to hear. Until he and Jess decided what to do with the hospital, its operation was their responsibility, and no way in hell did he want it staffed inadequately. For sure, it was an issue to address with Rick in the very near future. But in the meantime he was just another of the doctors in the field. A fact he became acutely aware of as he got closer to the accident scene, close enough to see the need but also close enough to be stopped by the firefighters.

There was a crush of mangled metal ahead of him. Somewhere in that carnage, there were also injured children. He thought about Molly for a moment as he made his way forward, trying to push past what had turned into a wall of firefighters.

"Sorry, sir. You can't go any farther," one of them yelled at him.

He did stop, did try to obey the order. But when

he saw the first injured and bloodied child being pulled from the van, and when he saw that child's parents rush forward, crying and frantic to get to their little boy yet being pushed back like everybody else, that was when the coldest chill he'd ever felt in his life hit him. No, Molly wasn't one of the children involved in this mess, for which he was incredibly grateful, but the utter dread of having your child involved in something like this and not knowing…*that* was the cold chill he felt. The one that told him, in this instance, he knew exactly what it felt like to be a father.

"We've got everybody out of the van now except one child, a little girl, and the firefighters aren't going to let us in until they have it better secured," Rick called to Rafe from across the commotion of several dozen people doing several dozen different things. Lights were being set up, boundaries being laid out to keep the growing crowd under control. Various medics and rescuers were working with patients in all sorts of different conditions. People were taking pictures, others were videotaping. A helicopter overhead was shining a spotlight down. Attempts were under way to get down a cliff to the car perched on a ledge below. The passengers inside were phoning that they were OK, but the frenetic effort to rescue them was still under way, and the growing concern that the car could easily topple on down sobered the thoughts of everybody on the scene.

All Rafe wanted to do was shove everybody back so he could go get that little girl who was still trapped in the van. But on his second and third attempt to get through, he was still being pushed back by the firefighters. "Look, Doc, I know you want to get at that child as much as we do, but right now we can't do it. Site's not stable enough yet, and you don't have any rescue experience, do you?"

Rafe swallowed hard. He'd criticized Jess for giving up medicine to become a firefighter. Criticized him more than once. But now he wished to God he had his brother's rescue experience. "Do you know anything about her condition?"

The firefighter shook his head. "Other than she's not conscious, and she's trapped…her arm, I've been told. Sorry I don't have anything else for you. But as soon as we think it's safe…"

Not the words he wanted to hear. Not the image he wanted in his mind, because he was thinking about Molly, seeing her as the child trapped inside, wondering what the trapped child's parents were doing, thinking, feeling right now.

Damn, he wished Jess was here. No way in hell his would brother have stood here, waiting, wondering. Jess was about action. Sometimes it was action Rafe didn't like. But that was who Jess was now, and Jess would have been down on his belly, crawling to get in there, no matter what anybody said. Of that, he had no doubt.

On impulse, he phoned his brother. "OK, so I know there's nothing you can do from where you are, but talk me through it. I'm going in, don't give a damn what they're telling me to do or not do. I can't stand here and wait while that kid might be dying, so I need some common sense shouting at me before I do it."

"Are you sure?" Jess asked. "Considering *everything*, are you sure you're the one who should be going in there? I mean, none of that has changed about you, has it?"

Rafe drew in a ragged breath. "No, none of that

has changed. I'm still claustrophobic as hell and I expect that once I get inside that van I'm going to experience claustrophobia in a way it's never been experienced before. But somebody's got to get that kid out of there, Jess."

"Then my best advice to you is to get someone else, big brother, because if you get in there and panic..."

"No one else, Jess. It's just me." Because he wasn't going to be stopped by the things that could happen, when the thing that *had* happened wasn't being attended to as fast as he wanted it to be. So, maybe he was impatient. Maybe he was totally wrong. But if that was Molly in there, he'd be ripping through chunks of steel with his bare hands to get at her no matter what anybody else was telling him to do. For somebody else's little girl he could do no less. "And I'm going in, so give me the condensed version of how to do this, or I'm going to have to figure it out on my own."

"Damn it, Rafe..." Jess heaved out an impatient, audible sigh. "I hate heroes."

"No, you don't," Rafe said softly. The love of Jess's life—she had been a heroine. And Jess, himself, was a hero. "And I'm not going to do anything you don't tell me to do. So, are you with me?"

"You have to tell me everything," Jess warned. "And if you feel a panic attack coming on..."

His brother referred to all those times when their old man had locked him in a closet. It had been the one underneath the front stairs. No room to stand, no room to stretch out. Basically, a cubby-hole with a padlocked door on the outside. He'd crouched in there, his muscles aching and cramping, scared to death of the dark and the creepy, crawly things he imagined in the dark, crying quietly, while his brother sat outside, talking to him, reassuring him that he wasn't alone. It had happened so many times Rafe had lost count, and the result was a bad case of claustrophobia. Jess knew, and Rafe appreciated his brother's concern. But he was going in anyway.

"And you don't know what to expect?" Jess asked, breaking Rafe away from his childhood flashbacks.

"Arm's trapped. She's unconscious."

"Can you do a field amputation in there, if you have to?"

He could, but he didn't want to think about it. "Yeah, if I have to. But it's the last option. So just get me in there so I can see what needs to be done. OK? I'll deal with everything else once I get to the girl."

"Fine. Have they popped out all the glass yet?" Jess asked.

"As far as I can tell, yes."

"Good, then click me off some pictures on your phone so I can see it."

"Don't have time," Rafe growled.

"Take the time anyway, Rafe. You're not going in blind, and if you think you are, I'm going to hang up on you right now and call the fire department and ask them to put you in restraints."

Rafe actually chuckled. He knew his brother, and that was exactly what Jess would do. "Fine, some pictures coming at you." From a distance, he clicked shots of the three sides he could see then sent them on to his brother. It only took a minute for Jess to assess the situation and respond.

"Disclaimer first. You should be leaving this to

the professionals. But that van's positioned to go over if you're not careful, Rafe."

"They can't let it go over because there's another car down on the ledge below it. People trapped."

"OK, then they're going to have to take it apart piece by piece."

"With the kid inside?" Rafe asked.

"No. The kid's got to come out, one way or another. And, Rafe, they're not going to wait too long on this since they have survivors down below."

"Meaning?"

"Meaning huge chance of field amputation. Get yourself ready for it if you do get in."

"You mean *when* I get in."

Jess laughed. "Cut from the same cloth, brother."

"I guess we are." And there were apologies to be made to Jess. But later. "So, tell me how to get in."

"Windshield. Whatever you do, keep to the left. Passenger's side. If you go to the right, the van's going to shift, and the integrity of some of the anchor ropes could be compromised. From what I see, the van looks stable enough right now, but when you add your weight and motion…anyway, stick to the passenger's side and you should be OK for this first part. Oh, and, Rafe, if you do anything dumb, like get yourself killed, just remember that the first person you're going to meet up with in heaven's probably going to be Aunt Grace, and she's not going to like seeing you there."

"Trust me, I have no intention of having a face to face with Aunt Grace today."

"You're not going in, are you?" Edie exclaimed.

"You've been eavesdropping?"

"Enough to know that you're joking about getting yourself killed."

"Nobody's getting killed. But I *am* going in." He held up his phone. "I've got good instruction. Jess is going to be with me."

"And you're not a firefighter, Rafe! They're still telling us to wait."

"But I've got a patient inside who can't wait." He held the phone back up to his ear. "Look, you'll hang on, won't you?"

"Not going anywhere," Jess said.

"Rafe," Edie cut in, "we've got plenty of injuries for you to deal with over there." She pointed to the triage area, where the accident victims were being staged according to the degree of their injuries. "Rick asked me to tell you they need your help."

He looked, saw the medical flurry. "Tell Rick I'm working on another patient right now, that I'll be over there as soon as I can."

"You tell him," Edie snapped, pulling a helmet on.

"What are you doing?" Rafe asked.

"Going in with you to get April. That's her name, by the way."

"No way in hell!"

Edie looked up at him, stared him straight in the eye, then spun around and marched straight to the van, forcibly shoving back the firefighter who tried to grab hold of her. Once there, she turned and waited for Rafe.

"You're not doing this, Edie!" he shouted, catching up to her and trying to wave off two firefighters coming his way.

"And you're not stopping me."

"I am," one of the firefighters said, stepping in front of Rafe. The name on his jacket identified him as Chief Will Brassard. "I'm stopping both of you."

"No, you're not," Rafe said patiently. "I've got a child trapped in there who could die, and you're not going to let that happen to her, are you? If you let me go in, it's *not* your responsibility—if you do, it is. Simple choice, in my opinion, Chief." He held up the phone. "You know my brother Jess? He's going in with me."

"You're as persuasive as your aunt was," Brassard said, stepping back.

"I'll take that as a compliment." Rafe rushed round the man to get to Edie's side.

"Or a curse," Brassard muttered. "Here's the deal. If we cut through the metal, it's going to take a while, and it may undo what we've done to stabilize the van. Also, because the kid's head is positioned so that cutting around her is going to be a risk, that's pretty much the last thing we want to do. That, plus the fact that she's coming to, and I'm not sure she's going to hold still for what we'd have to do. One of my men tried getting her out, but she was lodged in there tight. There's not much room to do anything."

"Did he see bleeding?"

"Some. Not excessive. He couldn't tell where it was coming from, and he was afraid to start probing and risk more complications."

Tamponade, where blood flow was stopped by a constriction created by an outside force. It was the first thing that came to Rafe's mind, and something he couldn't shake off as he prepared to go in. A tamponade could be a lifesaver but, if dislodged, could be a killer. Somehow, in such a serious situation, with a lack of blood…

"Look, Corbett, you're aware how dangerous this is. And I don't like the fact that you're not experienced in field rescue. But we may not have too much time left for this kid if we don't get something done fast, and if we need a field amputation—"

"Last option," Rafe interrupted.

"Or first, depending on what happens. Which is why I'd rather put a doctor in there on that than one of my firefighters. We're going to keep trying to get at her from out here, but in the worst-case scenario, we have an emergency…you're going to have to take her arm and get her the hell out of there fast. No time to argue with us. You'll just have to do it. Understood?"

Rafe nodded.

"Good. I'll give you your shot at this, but if you can't make it work, we're going to have to take that van apart piece by piece so it doesn't fall down on that car below here. Those people trapped down there are at risk, too. Meaning five minutes in and you amputate if you don't have another solution. So you've got your timeline. Five minutes, then we're pulling everybody out. And at that point, if the kid is still stuck, I'm putting one of my medics in to take her arm if you haven't already done it. So it's going to be your rescue, Doc. And also your choice." He tossed his helmet over to Rafe.

Five minutes. He was already feeling sweat drip down his back. Five minutes wasn't a lot of time to wait, but those five minutes could be precious to that child trapped in there. Especially as more than five minutes had already ticked off the clock since he'd been here, and at least thirty minutes beyond that. "I'm going in," he said to Edie.

"And I'm right behind you," she replied, then

thrust out her hand to stop him from arguing with her. "You're not stopping me, Rafe. If April wakes up…"

Edie was good at what she did. Brilliant, actually. But putting her into this kind of situation? "You'll do what I tell you," he warned her. "Your job…your only job…will be to keep her calm, and if she's not conscious, I want you out of there. Do you understand? You can't get in the way because I may have to…" He paused, swallowed hard. "May have to amputate her arm. You understand that, don't you?"

"I understand," she said. "And I'll do whatever you tell me to."

"Then let's do it." He held his phone back to his ear. "I'm going in. I'll keep this line open, but if something happens…" He didn't finish the sentence, didn't even wait to hear his brother's response. Instead, he got down on his belly and wormed his way through the broken-out windshield.

"What can you see?" Edie asked, wedged in tight against Rafe's back.

"First thing I can see is that there's no way in

hell I'm going to fit in here. Second thing I can see is that her arm is pinned in tight, and it's basically caught up in the mechanism of the seat that was in front of her. I don't see any blood so I want to get a blood-pressure reading, but I can't move." The forces of his own private hell were beginning to close in around him already. He was basically on the interior roof of the car, lying on his side, wedged in between two dislodged seats where there was barely enough room for his large frame to fit. Maneuvering in this tight space was nearly impossible. Catching his breath in the tightness closing in on his chest was nearly impossible as well. "Can you take a BP reading? I think we're going to have to trade places so you can do it, as there's no maneuvering room in here for a man my size."

Edie drew in a sharp breath, heard Rafe do the same. "Sure, I can do that," she said, already backing away so Rafe could scoot himself out and let her go in first.

"April," Edie said, on her way out. "Can you hear me?"

The child murmured a faint "Uh-huh."

"We're here to get you out, so don't be afraid." As she brushed by Rafe, she whispered, "Talk to her. Reassure her. The words don't matter as much as the fact that she's not alone here."

"How is it in there?" Rick called from outside.

"Tight," Edie yelled. "Her arm seems caught almost all the way to her shoulder, but it's hard to tell, and she's trapped at a difficult angle. Rafe's too large for the space." She glanced back in, aimed her flashlight into the interior dark space and saw Rafe talking to the child as he slid himself out.

"Well, once you get back in there, maybe you could…" Rick held out the blood-pressure cuff she needed, as well as an old teddy bear. "It used to be Christopher's."

"I think she'll be glad to have it," Edie said, dropping back to her knees, waiting for Rafe to make his exit.

"I'll be right back, April," Rafe reassured the child in a voice so tender it nearly broke Edie's heart. Somehow she had to make Rafe understand what an amazing father he'd make for Molly. She could see it so clearly. She thought Molly probably could, too. Rafe was the only one denying it, and she didn't know why. It bothered her, though, because where there could be so much happiness, Rafe was bound to a path that seemed like such a waste.

"Four minutes," Brassard stepped in and warned.

Rafe nodded, but didn't acknowledge him in any other way. "She's brave," he said to Edie, "but we're going to have to get her out of there pretty soon because I don't know what else is going on with her, and she's been pinned too long. Have you ever taken a blood pressure in somebody's leg before?"

Fear, icy cold and blinding, hit her. "No, but I can do it. Um…Rafe? Since *you* can't get in there, you won't expect me to…to amputate, will you? If that's what it comes down to, I won't have to be the one…?"

"It's not going to get to that," Rafe said. "I promise, Edie. We're going to find another way to get her out of there."

Reassuring words that didn't reassure her as much as she would have liked because her hands started to tremble and she couldn't stop them.

"Rafe, I…I'll do what I have to do. But I'm not sure…"

He reached out and took both her hands into his. "That's the last possible alternative, Edie. To save that child's life, if that's what it comes down to, I know you *can* do what you have to do. And I'll be right there with you. But we're going to look at other alternatives first. I'm not going to take that little girl's arm without exhausting every other possibility. I promise you." Ever so gently, he brushed a strand of hair back from her face. "I'll be with you, Edie, no matter what happens."

His voice was so calm, so reassuring she wanted to believe him. Something in Rafe inspired her to be more than she was, to see capabilities in herself more than she had. "I know you will," she whispered, fighting hard to keep the trembling out of her voice. "But I'm not sure if I can."

"My aunt trusted you with the ominous task of turning me into the father she thought I could be, and that speaks volumes. Actually, it shouts volumes."

"You know about that?"

"Of course I know about that." He tilted her

face up to his. "I trust you to help me, Edie, not because my aunt trusted you but because I trust you. You can do this…we can do this. But I won't force you to go back in there with me if you don't want to."

"When you get back in there, you've got three minutes," Brassard reminded them.

This time Edie paid no attention to the fire chief. "I'm going in *with* you, Rafe," she whispered, her voice still shaky. This was nothing she'd ever prepared herself to do, but Rafe gave her confidence. And that confidence grew as she felt Rafe right behind her on her way in. "Hi, April. My name is Edie, and I've come to help get you out of here. I know you're scared, so I brought you a little friend to hold on to while Dr. Rafe and I take care of you." April took hold of the bedraggled teddy with a fierceness that told Edie she was a tough little girl. "So, what I need to know first is where you hurt the most. Can you tell me?"

April nodded. "My arm. It's stuck. And there's something in my tummy, on the side."

Edie rolled a little to her left, wedged herself back against another of the seats that had broken loose, and aimed her flashlight at April. That was when she saw it…something wedged into the child's side, just above her waist. Maybe part of the metal bracing broken off one of the seats?

"Two more minutes," someone outside shouted.

"Rafe," Edie said calmly, trying not to alarm the child, "April has a tummyache. I think I can see the cause of it."

"Where?"

"Left side, just above her waist. Metal bar of some sort, I think. Wedged in, can't tell how deep." She waited for his response, waited for him to tell her what to do, but what she heard instead was an utterance of profanity under his breath. So she continued to talk to April. "Can you wiggle your fingers, April? Just your fingers, nothing else." Edie shifted the position of her flashlight so she could watch April's reaction, and what she saw for a moment was a child putting forth every effort she had—frowning, biting down on her lip, squeezing shut her eyes to concentrate.

"A little," April finally said, with great effort. "My thumb a little, and I think my first two fingers. My others feel…yucky."

"How yucky?" Edie asked instinctively.

"Like they're not there."

Edie cringed inwardly, and Rafe gave her a supportive squeeze on her shoulder. "Are they sticky?" he asked April.

"Some."

"And cold?" he continued.

"Yes. And they hurt all the way up my arm."

"Pain is a good sign," Rafe murmured into Edie's ear, then continued, "When we get her loose, we've got to stabilize the metal bar in her side before we move her out. Just make sure we don't bump it or dislodge it somehow."

Those words sent cold chills up Edie's spine, almost as much as Chief Brassard's one-minute warning did. "Let me get her BP before we do anything else, and maybe you can figure out how to take care of her arm in the meantime." She wedged herself in a little closer to the girl. "April, I've got to check your blood pressure. It's going to pinch a little, but it only lasts a few seconds. The reason we do this is so we know how well your heart is sending the blood flowing to all the places in your body it needs to go."

"So you can fix me up when I get my arm out?"

Edie felt a knot catch in her throat. That was what she wanted, what she was praying for, but the two things she'd never do were offer false hope or lie. Which was why she chose her words carefully. "So we can give you the best care when we get you out of here. OK?" The knot almost choked her as she spoke, but she was going to hold on to hope…because of Rafe. He would do everything possible to help this child, and to assure the best outcome. She believed that with all her heart.

"OK," April agreed. "But I'm getting sleepy. I want to go home."

Sleepy meant shock. With her limited medical training, Edie knew that, and it worried her. "Soon, sweetheart. We'll get you home as soon as we can. In the meantime, just try and hold as still as you can, and be very quiet, because I've got to listen through these." She held up the stethoscope, then impulsively placed them in April's ears and placed the bell on her own heart. "Can you hear it beating?"

"Yes," the girl said, almost mesmerized.

"That's what I'm going to be listening for in

you, only in a different place. I'll bet you didn't know that there are places all over our bodies where we can either feel your heartbeat or listen to it."

"Will you show me?" April asked, almost timidly.

"When we get you out of here, and after the doctors at the hospital have had a look at you, I will definitely show you. So…" She held a shushing finger to her lips then twisted slightly to look back at Rafe, who handed her the blood-pressure cuff.

"You're doing a good job," he whispered, as she took it from him.

She hoped so, hoped that wasn't just Rafe trying to be encouraging. "How do I do this? I know how to take a reading in the arm, but not in the leg."

"There's not much difference. It's all about the positioning. What you need to do first is bend the knee of her right leg, and try keeping her foot flat, without twisting her abdomen. Actually, let me move over a little so I can work with her foot."

He scooted back, brushing against her, and even in his slightest touch she felt his strength rush through her. Edie hoped her shiver was imperceptible to him, even though to her it was massive, shaking her down to her very essence. "So I strap on the cuff next?" she asked.

"Make sure the bottom is about an inch above April's ankle then put the stethoscope on the dorsalis pedis artery. Find that by placing your finger halfway between the inner ankle bone and the Achilles tendon. Let me know when you're there."

Knowing such a little thing may have seemed simple to Rafe, but to Edie his knowledge was awe-inspiring. "I feel it," she said, when she'd finally located the pulse.

"Good. Now listen. Most of the time you'll be able to hear it pretty easily. Sometimes, in about two to three percent of healthy people, the sound can't be heard in one or both legs, though. Pump up the cuff like you would in the arm, and listen."

Which was exactly what she did. "Ninety-four over fifty-six," she said, then heard an audible sigh of relief from Rafe.

"Time's up. Everybody out!" Brassard yelled.

Edie and Rafe both ignored the warning. "A little low but, all things considered, not bad," he finally said, as he reached over Edie and took the cuff and equipment. "Now, the next thing we need to do is pack some gauze around her abdominal would to make sure nothing moves." He handed several wads of gauze over to her. "Just be gentle. Build up enough around the metal bar so we reduce the risk of bumping it when we finally pull her out of there, then tape the gauze into place."

"I said, get out!" Brassard yelled.

"I like my job a whole lot better than I like yours," she said, placing the first of the gauze. Her fingers trembled, her gut churned. She bit down on her lower lip, concentrating so hard she could taste her own blood. "How will I know if it's good enough?"

Rafe gave her a little squeeze on the arm. "It'll be good enough, Edie. Trust me, you'll do a good job." His squeeze was a squeeze of triumph, maybe of relief…whatever it was, it caused her confidence to soar. Rafe was definitely in charge here, and one way or another, he would make things work for April.

"Get the hell out of there!" Brassard yelled

again. “Right now, or I’m sending in one of my men!”

They both ignored him again. “Well, I think I’ve got as much gauze taped in as I can. What’s next?”

“What’s next is that I’m going to go out and let Chief Brassard know he can’t start cutting. Not the van, not…” He nodded toward April. “I’m going to persuade him to give us more time. You going to be OK in here for a minute?”

“We’ll be fine,” Edie said, wiggling into a more comfortable position, grateful she wasn’t spooked by cramped spaces, because this was about as cramped as she’d even been in any space. Cramped and now dark.

“What’s it looking like in there?” Rick asked even before Rafe was all the way out.

“Child’s stable. Talking. Scared, but Edie’s handling that. Haven’t been able to evaluate her arm yet, but she does have some kind of a rod stuck through her belly, and as there’s no significant bleeding to go with it, I’m thinking tamponade.”

A diagnosis that caused Rick to suck in a sharp

breath. "Well, I'll get the OR ready for that one. And her arm..."

Rafe shrugged. "Don't know enough to give an educated guess at this point. But what I need for you to do is hold off the fire department for me. Don't know how, don't care, but there's no way in hell I want them taking that van apart, not when I've got a kid in there with a rod through her belly. And she's too alert to take off her arm, especially when I don't think it needs to come off. We need to find a way to get her out without jostling her, and while I know the guys out here are doing the best they can, there's got to be another way."

"Done," Rick said. "Anything else?"

"More light, if we can manage it."

"Done," Rick repeated.

Rafe would have asked for more space, but it didn't matter. For now he was stuck with a good case of claustrophobia, and there was nothing he could do about it. "Oh, and while I don't see anything to indicate it, prepare for crush syndrome, just in case. I have an idea we may get lucky with that one, but I don't want to get everything else right and have that go wrong on us." A smile twinkled in his eyes. "Oh, and if you have to cite crush syndrome to the fire chief as a reason why we *can't* rush getting April out of there, do it." Crush syndrome was where an extremity or other part of the body that has been trapped for a long time could start causing other problems throughout the body with the release of dangerous chemicals at high levels. Shock at the immediate release was almost always a given. Kidney failure could result, as well as death. It was a little devious using that because he was fairly certain April didn't have it, but any excuse in a storm. And crush syndrome was a good excuse. "Also, since I have every confidence that you're going to buy us more time, I'd like to get an IV started in April before we do *anything*." A tall order for a limited space. It was going to be a challenge.

"I'll get the supplies ready to go in. Oh, and Jess called. He hadn't heard from you, and his phone clicked off. Said to call him when it's over." He started to turn away from Rafe, but turned back. "I thought about it, by the way."

"What?"

"The apology, the offer."

"Now's a hell of a time to bring it up," Rafe said. "Especially if you want to negotiate something."

"No negotiation. Accepted. All of it."

In response, Rafe arched his eyebrows. "Light sedative, too," he said, then spun round and went straight back to the van.

"I think we need a better vantage point," Edie called out to him. "The extra lights are good, but I think we need to have a look at her arm, and do it from somewhere between the seat and the floor?"

"Then that's what I'll do," he said, gritting his teeth, knowing that he was going to have to shove himself into an opening where he didn't fit. "Look, Edie," he began once he was back in the van, "there's something I've got to tell you… something I hope to God doesn't cause any problems here." He paused a second, then continued. "I'm claustrophobic."

"A lot of people are."

"Not like me. I'm claustrophobic to the point of panic attacks. My old man used to lock me in a closet. Made me spend hours there. On a couple of occasions, days. Most of the time I'm OK dealing with it, but in tight spaces…"

Edie rolled over and squeezed Rafe's hand. "We'll deal with it," she said.

And that was all she had to say, because he knew they would. Together.

"It feels like the walls of hell are closing in on me," Rafe panted, slithering his way into a tiny space at the back of the seat. He couldn't see, didn't really fit, was sweating in a way he'd never sweated before, and holding his breath in such long spurts his lungs were beginning to hurt. His lip was bleeding from biting down so hard, his muscles already aching from extreme clenching, and the panic headache pummeling him had such a loud, thumping beat to it he was surprised Edie couldn't hear it. But after five minutes he'd cut away significant snippets of seat, and for that he was relieved. April was still doing well. Sleeping now, with an IV anchored in her leg, and a small amount of sedative to keep her relaxed.

"You OK?" Edie asked for the hundredth time.

"I'd rather be eating a baguette at Le Pain

Merveilleux in Paris. But as that's not an option, I'm doing fine."

"You've been to Paris?"

He reached up to cut away another strip of seat vinyl then rose up and shone a light down into the seat's exposed innards. "Twice. The first time was all work, no play. Medical conference. Second time I decided that all work really wasn't the best thing to be doing in Paris, so I indulged in some of the finer things…the wine, the museums, the food…"

"The women?" she asked.

He chuckled. "As lovely as the women of Paris are, and they are some of the most beautiful in the world, I decided to make it an adventure for one. It's easier that way. No one to fight with over where to go or what to do. No one to tell me when to take a nap if I wanted one, or not to drink so much wine, if that's what I had a mind to do. Doing Paris as a single really wasn't so bad," he said, pulling himself into a better angle and fighting off the panic that wanted to slap him down the instant he realized he was stuck in there as tight as humanly possible, with nowhere to go, or even move, unless he wanted to back out. At this point, he was in so tight he wasn't sure he could even do that.

"But wouldn't it have been wonderful to do Paris with someone you loved, someone you could share the adventure with, who didn't care about your naps, or drinking too much wine?"

"Maybe," he said, feeling an increase in his heart rate, feeling the tightening of his muscles, as each and every one started clamping down on him in some kind of conspiracy. No air to breathe… He tried, sucked it in greedily. Shut his eyes, tried to focus. "If that person…existed. But she…doesn't. At least not…for…me."

"So you're an avowed bachelor?" she continued. "I mean, I understand the no-dating thing. But no nothing? Not ever?"

"Something like that," he forced out, sounding winded.

"But wouldn't an avowed bachelor still like some consistency in his life? Maybe not in the form of a wife, or even a permanent adult relationship, but what about a child? They keep you young, you know. Change your focus. Give you balance. Make you more giving, I think."

Why the hell was she prattling on about this now? He was in the throes of a damned panic attack, and she was starting up on him adopting Molly.

"Can you even imagine the sense of accomplishment you could feel once you've raised that child, and she's turned out to do something huge, like invent the drug that will cure cancer, or teach the world how to achieve global peace? I mean, one little child, in the right home situation, with the right parent, could do so much…"

He shut his eyes for a moment, reined in his anger. She had him trapped—now she was doing the hard adoption sell. "I can't raise Molly, if that's what this is about. I've told you that. I can't… *won't* do it."

"Even though you're bound to be desperately lonely in your old age, considering the way you isolate yourself?"

"My choice. I isolate myself because that's what I choose to do."

"And who knows how you'd feel if you opened

up a little, took Molly in, raised her as your daughter? She's a wonderful little girl, Rafe. Give yourself some time to get to know her, and I promise you'll see how fantastic she is. She'll make you better in ways you've never thought could happen."

He glanced down into the seat parts and saw… was that April's hand? Quickly, he shifted slightly and repositioned the flashlight for a better look. "I know she's a wonderful little girl, and I know that adopting her is what everyone wants me to do, but…" He pressed himself tighter into the seat until the edge of it nearly cut off his breathing. "I see it," he said. "Her hand, her arm…I can see the whole thing. And… Thank God for small miracles. Her arm is fine. It's only her hand that's trapped, and I think… Hand me the oil, Edie."

She handed him a bottle of lubricant that had come in with several other medical supplies then positioned a flashlight from her place down below. "I've got the IV steady, and I'm holding on to April, supporting her belly so that metal rod doesn't move, so do what you have to do."

Which was what he did. He maneuvered April's

hand out of its trap. Gently released each of her fingers, one by one, then moved on down the hand until he'd finally extricated her wrist. No words spoken, no whispers, no gasps. Simply swift efficiency when it was clear what was required of him to assure that April Crowley's life was going to go forward beautifully, after a fair amount of reconstructive surgery and rehabilitation.

Five minutes after extricating April's arm, he handed her out to the waiting medics, the metal bar still holding its place in her belly, then crawled out himself and collapsed on the ground, grateful to inhale unobstructed breaths, grateful for all the open space around him.

"You OK?" Edie asked, plopping down beside him. For a moment they were two people lying flat on the ground, staring up at the night sky, while the rest of the medical emergency whirled on around them. The only two people…

"Fine," he said. "You?"

"What we did in there, Rafe…I can't even…"

"No words to describe it?"

"No words."

But actions spoke louder than words as he

reached across and took hold of Edie's hand, then simply held it for the next minute or two. Or for an eternity. It all seemed the same right then. And it all seemed very good.

CHAPTER SEVEN

OK, IT WAS only a kiss. Well, maybe a little more than a kiss. Or something on the way to becoming a whole lot more. He'd kissed plenty of women in his time, no big deal. But two days after the bus accident, two grueling days of taking care of a sick little girl who didn't want to stay in bed or follow doctor's orders, and that kiss was still on his mind. That made it a big deal, didn't it?

The heck of it was he didn't know why. Or maybe he didn't want to dig deeply enough to find out why. Either way, he was grateful for the routine his life had settled into in the interim. Take care of Molly, rest, take care of Molly. For someone sick, she sure had a lot of energy. Even though Edie had warned him, he hadn't expected it, didn't know what to do with it and, in so many profound ways, it scared him. This child needed so much, and in ways he couldn't even begin to fathom.

In his defense, amidst his obvious lack of parenting skills, he hadn't run short of patience yet. That surprised him. But some of that had to do with Edie, who stopped by before work every day, and had spent the evenings there after her workday had ended. She'd cooked, read to Molly, played games. It was a sight to behold, a glimpse of life he'd never before seen. Family life at its best. Which simply reaffirmed to him who needed to be a family. At times, though, when he caught himself observing that family life too closely, his realization turned to cold chills. Could this be what he really wanted?

Reality always slammed back. This *wasn't* his life. Couldn't be. He wasn't going to let himself buy in to some ridiculous delusion that he could ever have it, because that wasn't meant to be the case. He was his father's son, after all. Corbett blood at its very worst. No getting around it. "French toast?" he asked Edie. "Is that what you're fixing?"

"Molly requested it, along with fresh strawberries."

"Do you think she might be taking advantage

of this situation? I know she's been sick, but that doesn't necessarily mean she should be wrapping you round her little finger."

"And if she is, does it matter?" Edie arranged the strips of toast on a plate, then put the plate on a serving tray. "We all need to be indulged sometimes, Rafe. Too bad most of us only get it in some kind of a crisis. And as far as being wrapped round her little finger, I don't think that's really possible if you enjoy what you're doing for someone."

"Well, I'm not sure being overly indulgent is the best thing to do. Most of us never get it at all. But then the other side of that coin is who really needs it? It spoils us for something we can't have all the time. Or in some cases won't have ever again. Why put yourself through that emotional mess"

"Emotional mess? How do you consider that being indulged a little leads to an emotional mess?"

"Because being indulged leads to expectations, most of which can't ever be met. At least not on practical or consistent terms. So call it pragmatism if you want. Or pessimism. Either way, the result is the same. I mean, what's the definition of indulgence anyway? To take unrestrained pleasure in? To gratify? If you want it, do it. It's just that easy. Well, guess what? You don't have to depend on someone else to do it for you. In fact, why bother? They may not meet your expectations or needs, so just go and indulge yourself."

"Sounds like someone needs some indulging himself," Edie responded. "Did you get up on the wrong side of the bed this morning?"

"What I need is my life back. Not this pseudo-domesticity." Because the closer he came to domestic, the more he wanted it. And the more he wanted it, the more he knew he couldn't have it. Which was why he was grumpy this morning, the side of the bed on which he'd woken up notwithstanding. Seeing Edie in the kitchen, fixing breakfast for Molly, seeming so happy in that place… all he wanted to do was shove his fist through the wall. Which proved that his old man could get through any time, any place. With so little provocation, too. "I need to find Molly a family then go home and get back to doing what I do best. It's as simple as that."

"Is it really that simple, Rafe? Giving up a child seems anything but simple to me. In fact, I think it'll be the hardest thing you'll ever have to do… if you really intend to go through with it."

"Oh, I intend to." He drew in a deep, steadying breath in the hope of warding off some of the agitation that seemed to be filling him up. "And, Edie? Just so you'll know, what's simple is the desire. The rest of it is getting pretty damned complicated."

"Then uncomplicate it. Adopt her."

"Well, isn't that just a wealth of insightful advice. Adopt her and do what? Tell me, Edie. What, exactly, should I do with Molly once I adopt her? I won't have time for her. So maybe I can shuffle her off to boarding school. And I don't have experience with children. So maybe I can hire her a full-time nanny, governess, tutor or whatever other kinds of child-care specialists money can buy to raise her the right way. Are either of those acceptable solutions? Because they're all I have. And just so you'll notice, neither one of those come with a full investment of me, because I'm really not adding much of myself to the deal."

Damn, he didn't mean to snap at her, didn't mean to be so grumpy. And he certainly wouldn't do any of the things he'd just said. But he couldn't get Edie to see the situation for what it was. And right now, existing so close to everything he truly wanted yet wasn't able to have was taking its toll on him. Two days of playing father had made him realize he wanted it probably more than anything he'd ever wanted. But two days had also reminded him why he had to back away. And fast.

"I was right. You do need some indulging."

He'd expected another fight from her, but got sympathy instead. He wasn't sure what to do with that. Wasn't sure he wanted to find out. "Look, I'm sorry for snapping. I'm sorry for being so disagreeable. But this whole domestic thing…it's not working for me."

"Or it's working too well. Have you ever considered that?"

He stared at her for a moment, amazed by the insight and annoyed by it at the same time. To have someone read him the way Edie did made him feel so vulnerable he was almost shaking. He wasn't going to be vulnerable, not to anyone, for any reason. That was the way it was, the way it had to be. "Look, you need to get to work. How about I take this tray up to Molly so you won't be late?"

"You really work hard at keeping people at arm's length, don't you?" She handed him the tray. "I don't think it comes naturally to you, Rafe. I think you want to let people in, but once they get close, you get scared."

"So, with French toast I get psychoanalysis, whether or not I want it?"

"Point taken. It's none of my business."

She was right, though. He did keep people at a distance. Even people he wanted to let in, like her. "Look, Edie. I really appreciate all the help you've been with Molly these past couple of days, and I'm sorry about my rotten attitude. It gets away from me sometimes."

"It's not as rotten as you think, Rafe. More like, it's honest. I don't necessarily agree with you, pretty much in most things that concern Molly, even in some of the things you think about yourself. But we're all welcome to our opinions, aren't we? No matter how right or wrong they may be."

He chuckled. "And that implies that my attitude is wrong?"

She tossed him a cheery smile. "It implies whatever you want to make of it. Now, go and take care of Molly."

She'd shooed him out the kitchen door before he could respond in a semi-intelligent way, but there was something about being around Edie that caught him off guard more than he wanted to be. And by the time Molly had eaten as much of her breakfast as she cared to, Edie appeared upstairs with another tray bearing a plate of French toast and a bowl of strawberries. "Rafey needs someone to indulge him," she said to Molly, who was already involved in a video game.

Molly looked up at him. "Do you?" she asked, as if she totally understood what that meant.

"What I need has nothing to do with being indulged," he said, "and as you get older, and have more experience in life, you'll understand how meaningless it is. The indulgence lasts a minute, maybe two, then you're right back where you started, with a couple of minutes you'll never be able to get back again. And a longing that may never be satisfied."

"But it has French toast with it," Molly argued. "And Edie makes the best French toast ever!"

Something in Molly's simplicity struck a chord with him. Or made his position seem awfully rigid. "So, do you think I ought to go indulge myself?" he asked.

Molly nodded. "But only if you like French toast."

In a way, it made perfect sense to him. And as he crossed the room to take the tray from Edie, she shook her head.

"Not here. This morning you get breakfast in bed. The ultimate of all indulgences."

"Why?" he asked, clearly puzzled by the attention.

"Because you never have. Because it's time."

She was right. He'd never had breakfast in bed. There was no reason to when a quick cup of coffee and a muffin from one of the hordes of coffee shops would suffice. "Why is it time?" he asked, intrigued.

"When I was young, I loved making breakfast and serving it in bed to my mother. Especially when she wasn't sick. I think it made her feel like she was special, like she really mattered. Like she wasn't a burden to me. And it always seemed to bring us a little closer. Taking care of other people does that, Rafe. It's who I am. So, which bedroom is yours?"

"You're serious about this?"

"I sliced every one of these strawberries myself. That makes me pretty darned serious, don't you think?"

Serious, and sexy, and more frightening than he'd bargained for. Because, for the first time in his life, he wanted that breakfast in bed, wanted to be indulged. Maybe because he knew it was a genuine, generous offer and not one that could come back to bite him in some unknown way.

Leading Edie to the bedroom he was using, he stopped short of the door and turned to face her. "My father would offer a cookie, or a candy bar, or some other thing that a little boy would truly want, then he'd tell me to come and take it from his hand. 'Come on, Rafe. You can do it. Just take this cookie…' Sometimes he'd give it to me, and sometimes he'd hit me. The hell of it was, I never could tell what he was going to do. After so many years of his abuse, you'd have thought I could figure it out, but…"

"But you were always that little boy who hoped his dad would hand him the cookie and never hit him again. I'm so sorry…"

He shook his head. "It made me stronger."

"And less trusting."

"But don't *you* have a motive with this French toast? Be nice to me, indulge me a little, and maybe weaken my position on what I'm going to do with Molly? You may not slap me, Edie, but what's the difference?"

"The difference is, sometimes a nice gesture is just that…a nice gesture. I'm sorry you got slapped, Rafe, but I wasn't the one who slapped you." She shoved the tray at him. "I think maybe I shouldn't come back any more. When Molly's allowed out of the house, I'd like to spend some time with her. Not like this, though." She turned, and walked out the door. In the hall, however, she stopped, and turned back to face him. "Some-

times French toast is just French toast, Rafe.
yours is cold now." Then, spinning on her
she marched away.

It hadn't been a good parting and, truthfully
missed him. Missed Molly, too. But she'd ste
over the line. Gotten involved where she shou
have, and now she had to live with the outc
Meaning she'd let Grace down in a huge
She should have stayed detached, shouldn't
kissed him, or made him that silly French t
But she had, and that was that. No going b
Rafe was going to do what he wanted and she
no longer involved with any of it. Or with
In fact, this morning, when she'd mustered
courage to call him, he hadn't even bothered
swering. Or returning a call later on. And no
the end of the day, she was no longer jumpin
each and every incoming call, hoping it was

"Why the glum expression?" Rick asked
passing. "Your day's over. I'd think you'd
happy to leave here."

"Just reflecting on all the mistakes I've m
in my life."

He chuckled. "Well, after you've reflected on yours, if you need a few more to work out, come see me. I've got a pretty long list, topped by a couple of whoppers."

"The thing is, when you're involved in the act that ultimately turns out to be a mistake, you can't see that it's a mistake. You go into it clear-headed, plunge all the way through it, and it's only when you come out on the other end that you realize what you've done. Good intentions aside, wouldn't it be smarter if people didn't get so involved in things that didn't concern them?"

"Smarter, maybe. But wouldn't it be a dull life if we didn't get involved, from time to time, where we shouldn't? It's a growing experience, Edie. Sometimes good growth, sometimes difficult growth."

"Well, maybe I'm not in the growing mood."

"Then you should stay locked in your office. Text or email only when necessary and, for heaven's sake, don't answer your phone."

In spite of her bad mood, she laughed. He was right, of course. "Look, I didn't mean to dump my problems on you."

"In case you didn't notice, I was the one who commented on your glum expression. You know, getting involved in a place I probably don't belong. But on the off chance that I might be able to help you work out this mistake you think you've made, can I?"

"Maybe the better question is, can I?" Could she simply walk up to Rafe's door, tell him she would back off? Tell him that Molly was his decision and she was no longer going to interfere?

"Well, whatever you do, tell Rafe to call me. I need to finish up some paperwork about his involvement in the rescue the other day, and get him to sign off on it. But he's not answering his phone."

"Not for you, either?"

"Rafe…he's the big mistake you're talking about, isn't he?"

"What makes you think that? We're barely friends. I hardly know him." Even as she said the words, she felt the blush creeping to her cheeks.

"And you wear your heart on your sleeve, Edie. That's what makes you so good with the kids. You care, they see it, they feel it. There's nothing hidden. Which goes for Rafe, too. Nothing hidden."

"It's not what you think."

"Or maybe it's not what *you* think. Look, at the risk of getting involved in a place I shouldn't, let me just tell you one thing. Years ago I took my shot at it. The timing was bad, my self-esteem shot all to hell, and I went in a direction I later regretted for more reasons than I've got time to tell you about. But out of that confusion, out of that bad place in my life and all the mistakes I was making, I got my son, and he's my constant reminder that there's nothing that can't be fixed if we want to fix it. Rafe and I…we've had problems in the past. Rafe came to me, apologized, and I was the one who wasn't ready to deal with it, wasn't ready to let those mistakes…his and mine…pass. Yet when I go home at night, and see Christopher…" He smiled, shook his head. "The best things in life can happen when you're least expecting them. Even in the midst of what you think is the worst mistake you've ever made. Like I said, you wear your heart on your sleeve.

That's not a mistake, Edie. So, tell him to give me a buzz when he has time."

"He's not easy, Rick."

"Want to see the scar on my shin to prove it?" he asked. "Of course, if you ever notice a little nick on his right shoulder..." He grinned. "In the meantime, I've got a pizza date with a very demanding little guy who rocks my world. No mistake, Edie. In the whole scheme of the universe, definitely no mistake."

So maybe it wouldn't be a mistake, dropping by to see Rafe and Molly. That was the resolve that got her all the way up to the driveway. But the rest of the way, from the road to the door, after her resolve had dissolved, she doubted herself in every way she possibly could. She didn't want involvement, yet she did. She craved it while she pushed it away. Denied it while she dreamt of it. One way or another, she had to get her head straight. Get him totally out of it, or find a way to deal with how he was totally in it. She didn't know which, didn't want to know why she didn't want to know. It was all too confusing. And the plan had been so simple. Show Rafe that he could be Molly's father.

Well, in that, she'd failed. If anything, her insistence had caused more of a gap between them, pushed Rafe even further away from Molly than he had been before. Now it was time to see if she could fix it. Yet, as she rang the doorbell then stood there chewing away nervously on her bottom lip, waiting to be let in, she didn't have a clue in this world how she was going to accomplish that.

Step one foot inside, she told herself. Then take another step after that. And another, and another. That was all her brain would allow and she hoped against hope that her brain would come up with the second part of the plan once the first part was under way. Otherwise she'd be adding another mistake to her list, but with no good outcome in sight.

When the door opened a crack, Edie was prepared to meet Rafe eye to eye. But it wasn't Rafe there to let her in. "Edie!" Molly cried, practically jumping into her arms.

"You're looking better," Edie said, bending down to hug her. "Are you feeling better?"

"I have to, since I'm going to be a nurse."

"Nurse? That's a very good thing to be," she said, stepping inside and looking around. "In a few years, when you're old enough…"

"Not then. Now! I have to be a nurse now."

"Why now?" Edie asked.

Molly pointed to the kitchen. "Rafey's at the kitchen table, taking his nap. I think he's sick."

Suddenly Edie was alarmed. Darting around Molly, Edie ran straight to the kitchen where Rafe was, indeed, slumped over the kitchen table. His face in his arms, breathing, thank God. "Rafe," she said, laying her fingers to the pulse in his neck.

"I'm alive," he muttered. "Wish I weren't, but I am."

He looked up at her through bloodshot eyes, and his features were hardly noticeable under a two-day growth of beard. Sexy, actually. Would have been sexier if he hadn't looked so darned sick.

"Would you mind making me some French toast?" he continued, his voice gravelly to the point it was beyond recognition. "I think I need someone to indulge me."

"Flu?" she asked, nudging him up, out of the chair. Getting a steadying arm around him, she guided him to the stairs.

"The worst flu anybody has ever had," he muttered, slumping into her as hard as he could without knocking her over.

Edie laughed. So she wore her heart on her sleeve? Well, if she did, the man leaning on her sleeve, maybe even drooling on it, was the man she loved. She wasn't sure what to do about it, except put him to bed.

"It's juice," Molly piped up. "You have to drink it. Edie said so."

Rafe glanced across the room, caught sight of his face in the mirror, and moaned. This was the first time he'd been sick in years. He hadn't caught so much as a cold, but look at him now. He was pale, emaciated looking, his eyes looked hollow. And Edie was loving every minute of it.

Actually, the part about Edie being here to take care of him wasn't all that bad. She was taking a few vacation days from the hospital to play nurse. It was nice. Domestic in a way that felt good. Probably too good, because he wasn't in much of a hurry for this little illness to come to an end. "Tell Edie I said thank you. And thank you, too, Nurse Molly." She was cute, carrying her play nurse's kit, dispensing him candy pills every hour. Edie had bought those for her, and managed to find a nurse's cap and surgical mask at the hospital, which Molly hadn't taken off for two days.

Oh, he was pretty sure it was all part of Edie's plot to get him to keep Molly, but the more he got to know the child, the more he knew she needed the best life she could possibly have, and parents who weren't…him.

At times, though, he did catch himself wishing it could be different.

"Edie said you have to get out of bed, get dressed and go and sit outside on the veranda for lunch. That your in-in…"

"Indulgence?"

She nodded. "It's over."

No wonder everybody at the hospital loved

Molly. No wonder his aunt had. She was a real charmer.

Thirty minutes later, Rafe descended the stairs, showered but not shaved. "It's a look," Edie said, fighting back a laugh. "Beard's good, but the sad look on your face sort of spoils the rugged effect."

"You're enjoying this, aren't you?"

"Not enjoying it so much as being entertained by it."

"My inconvenience is your entertainment?"

She shrugged. "Just a little. Oh, and so you'll know, it's only going to be the two of us for lunch. Johnny Redmond stopped by, and he's taken Molly with him to pick up a neglected pony out near Jasper. She was getting pretty restless being cooped up here, and I thought the fresh air would do her some good. Plus Johnny as much as promised her the pony would be hers once the pony is in better shape. Grace was in the process of trying to get this particular pony when she… Anyway, I guess it's a gentle thing, and there was no way Molly wasn't going out with Johnny to get it. Oh, and your brother called. He was surprised you were still here, and when I told him why, he said to say tough luck, but he's not coming back until you're over your flu."

"My family has an uncanny way of avoiding the things that really shouldn't be avoided."

"You mean the decision about Molly?"

"I mean decisions about a lot of things." His life, the hospital, Edie. *Molly.* "Look, would you like to take a walk with me?"

"Are you sure you're up to it?"

"I'm fine. More humiliated about my illness than anything else."

Edie laughed. "Just proves you're human, like the rest of us. You had the same flu as Molly, who came through it in good spirits."

"Children take things better. They don't have as many preconceived ideas of how they really should be feeling."

"If you say so."

"And illnesses usually run a much less serious course with children."

"Anything you say, *Doctor.*" Smiling, she turned to face him. "But keep in mind I'm the one who works with sick children, so if it's me you're trying to fool…"

"Not trying to fool, Edie," he said, suddenly serious. "In a way, that's what I've been doing. But I can't do it, not any longer."

"Fooling me about what?" she asked, stopping dead on the porch. "What's this about, Rafe? Molly?"

He nodded. "About adopting Molly."

"You're going to do it? You've actually decided to go through with it?" She was so excited she was almost jumping up and down.

"Not me, Edie. It's never been me, and I've said that all along."

"Then who?"

"You. I want you to adopt her. She loves you, you love her…"

Edie held out her hand to stop him. "No," she choked. "I can't do that. Grace wanted you—"

"And Aunt Grace isn't going to get everything she wanted. I'm sorry about that, and nobody wishes more than I do that it could have turned out differently. But I'm not the answer to this situation. You are. Which is why I want you to adopt Molly."

"But you, Rafe…"

He laid a hand on her arm. "Just listen to me for a minute, OK? Then maybe you'll understand why I can't do it. And believe me when I tell you I've given this a lot of thought. Lost sleep over it. Weighed it from every angle. Always came to the same conclusion."

"That I'm the one?"

"That you're meant to be Molly's mother. It makes sense. When I watch the two of you… Edie, my old man…" He paused for a moment, and stared off in the distance, at the property directly across the street. "We lived over there. Nice house. Big. Our house was actually nicer than Gracie House, if you go by size and furnishings." Except now it was a meadow. Trees, grass, several of Gracie Foundation's horses turned out to graze. For which he was very grateful. Land where so much hatred had been rooted deserved to be reclaimed for something good and decent.

"When the old man died, Jess and I burned it down. Didn't want to see it, didn't want it cluttering up the landscape as an ugly reminder. So we torched it…legally. Funny thing is, the town turned out and most of the people were shocked by our sentiment. Shocked that we would dare destroy the residence of the venerable Dr. Lawrence Corbett, but for us it was liberating. And what I discovered that day was that sometimes you have to dive into the fire in order to come out tempered on the other side. When I walked away, I didn't look back, didn't come back."

"No one ever knew, or suspected, what he'd done to you?"

"There weren't any visible scars to show anybody. Anything other than that was my word against his, and who the hell would believe a kid? Especially when that kid's father makes a point of telling everybody how bad his kid is."

"But your aunt?"

"She knew. But every time she threatened to turn him in to the authorities, he told her she'd better make sure she came out on top because if she didn't she'd never see Jess and me again. That was the one threat that always beat her, because if she had waged the battle and lost, I don't know what would have happened to Jess and me. Maybe the old man wouldn't have gone through with his threats but, then again, maybe he would have. Who knows?

"And whatever the case, Aunt Grace did what she had to do to stay involved in our lives. That's why she built her house across the road from ours. It wasn't so much that she wanted to live in Lilly Lake but she wouldn't live anywhere where my brother and I couldn't get to her whenever we needed to. And there were so many times…" He stopped. "But that's not why we're out here, is it? This is supposed to be about going on a nice walk, relaxing, thinking positive thoughts. About me telling you why I think you're the perfect mother for Molly."

But what positive thoughts could there be when every time Rafe stepped out the door he saw *the house*, even if, quite literally, it wasn't standing there any more? It looked like an innocent, peaceful lot, but the more Edie stared at it, the more she could see the house, see the scared little boys inside. For the first time, Edie truly understood why Rafe couldn't stay here. Memories adjusted, and they found their rightful place, but some memories didn't fade. To Rafe, the house was as real right now as it had been when he'd been a boy. All she had to do was look at the sadness written all over his face to know that, to understand it.

Perhaps it was when she studied the lines of that sadness that she realized she couldn't stay here and have him, too. The thing was, it was too soon to be thinking this way. She was only now discovering who she wanted to be, and the journey was good. Difficult, sometimes frustrating, but ultimately very good, and she wasn't ready to trade it in for anything else. Except maybe for motherhood? And perhaps for the slim chance at a life with someone who didn't have a clue where his own journey was taking him?

"I do love Molly," she confessed.

"Which is why I want you to take Gracie House. Adopt Molly, live here with her, give her the life she deserves."

So, this didn't come with Rafe after all. He was bargaining for his escape without taking anyone with him. And here she'd been, ready to make a commitment he had no intention of making himself. What a fool she'd been. An utter fool!

Still, she couldn't deny that stirring inside her.

Couldn't ignore it either. Because it was now infused with heartbreak…something she would never let him see. Which was why, when Rafe took hold of her hand and they headed toward the trail that led to the lake, she clung to him like her life depended on it yet didn't say a word. After all, what was there to say? Except… "No. I can't adopt her, Rafe. I'm sorry, but I can't adopt her."

Not because she didn't want to, because she did. With all her heart. But because Rafe was using her as his easy way out, and if he didn't have *her* to fall back on, maybe he would be the one to adopt Molly. With the way her heart was breaking, it was the only thing that made sense. The only thing she could do.

CHAPTER EIGHT

"I APPRECIATE you doing this for me. I'm usually a pretty good judge of character, but as this is about Molly, not me, I want your opinion of these people, too. Molly needs the best and I think you're much better equipped to handle that than I am."

Even before she entered the den where prospective adoptive parents Wallace and Betsy Cunningham were waiting, Edie felt a cold chill. She hated doing this. Hated, loathed, despised it. Couldn't believe he was actually going through with it. Somehow she'd hoped for a change of heart. But that wasn't the case. Rafe was actively interviewing prospective parents now, and the only thing she could feel was…nauseated. "Let's just get it over with," she said grumpily, on the first thud of what she knew was going to turn into a pounding headache.

"OK, I get it. You're not happy about my decision, but I still think it's best for Molly. She needs a real family. Needs the stability of parents who know how to raise a child, and that's not me. Apparently, not you either."

"That's not fair, Rafe. This was never supposed to be about me, and you know that!"

"What I know is that you turned me down, so I had to move on to the next plan."

"And do what? Hope that I'll back down and agree to take her when it looks like you're getting close to making a selection? Is that what this is about?"

"It's about moving on, Edie. We all need to do it, I think."

She'd peeked in at the Cunninghams a while ago. Peeked in at the Bensons as well as the Farleighs. They all seemed nice. Henry Danforth had put them through the initial wringers, so to speak, and she'd even read the background checks. All suitable candidates was what Henry had said. But Molly didn't need a suitable candidate. She needed a parent, or a set of parents.

The thing that bothered her most, though, was the air of indifference Rafe was trying to put on.

It wasn't working on him. She saw that, but she didn't know how to get through it. So maybe it was time…time to make the next move. She'd thought about it for two days now. In fact, that was all she'd thought about. Being Molly's mother. Even now, as the words floated through her mind, they made her smile. There was no downside to the situation. Not the way Rafe saw the downside, anyway. She loved Molly, and that was really all that mattered.

But it did feel like such a betrayal. Except the one thing that kept coming back to her was how Grace's only concern was that Molly have the best chance at a good life, with a good parent. So maybe Grace had miscalculated a little. Maybe what she had seen in Rafe simply wasn't there. The only thing was, Edie saw it in him, too. In those unguarded moments when he took hold of Molly's hand, when Molly walked next to him and tried to match his steps and Rafe would slow his stride just for her, in the way he watched Molly when he thought no one was looking…the big gestures didn't matter so much, but she saw Rafe's feelings for Molly in the little gestures.

She didn't know what to do, though. Not any more. "Yes, I think we all do need to move on," she finally responded.

Expelling a frustrated breath, Rafe turned away from the door to face Edie. "Look, I'm not going to argue with you about this. I thought it was going to be easy, finding her a family. In my mind, the perfect family would magically materialize, and Molly would get her happily-ever-after. I want her to have that, Edie. I *really* want her to have that."

"Yet you can't be the one to give it to her? Because she's getting attached to you, Rafe. I see it more and more every day. Molly adores you, and her attachment is growing."

He shook his head. "I see it too, and it scares the hell out of me. But, no, I can't be the one to bring her up. I know that makes me look terrible, but it's not me. I don't have what it takes to be a good father, and at least I have the sense to know what I'm *not* capable of doing. I wish it was different, but it's not."

But he wished he could raise Molly. Edie could see it in his eyes. Rafe truly wished he could, and something was stopping him.

"So, let's just get this over with, OK? Henry has one more set of prospective parents to send over later today, and by tonight I really intend on deciding which ones will get Molly."

"Which ones will *get* Molly? Will *get* Molly? Oh, my God, Rafe! Could you be any colder about it? It's like you're having a contest and she's the prize. Step right up, put your name in the hat, let me pick a winner!" OK, so she was shouting. She couldn't help it.

"Now you're being ridiculous," he hissed.

"I'm being ridiculous? Look in the mirror, Rafe. Take a good hard look then come back and tell me who's being ridiculous. Molly needs you, you need Molly, and I don't know why you can't see that. Everybody else can."

"Everybody else sees what they want to see, and you…you're the queen of it, Edie. But guess what, you're not seeing everything. You're not seeing why—"

"Then tell me, Rafe! Tell my why you're refusing to keep Molly. You keep saying that it's not your lifestyle, that you don't have room in your life, but I don't buy it. I've seen the way you and

Molly are with each other, and there's nothing in you that *doesn't* scream father." Her voice softened, and she reached out to squeeze his arm. "Rafe, please..."

He shook his head.

"Then I'll adopt her." She didn't want it to sound like she was accepting the consolation prize, because as she said the words, her heart skipped a beat. In the blink of an eye, she'd become a mother...Molly's mother. And suddenly she was excited. "I'll adopt her!" she said, the enthusiasm rising in her voice.

"You're sure about his?" he asked, sounding more relieved than anything else. "I've always thought it was the perfect solution, but I don't want to force you..."

"You're not forcing me, Rafe. I *do* want to adopt Molly. I want to be her mother, want to give her the home she needs. More than anything else, Rafe, I want to be the person who will help her develop into everything she's meant to be." The way *her* mother had done for her in spite of so much adversity. "I was lucky. I had a perfect mother who showed me life in so many wonderful ways.

That's what I want to be for Molly. What I want to do for Molly."

"Then Molly's going to be a very lucky little girl. From the moment I first laid eyes on you, I considered you perfect for Molly. She lights up around you…"

"She lights up around you, too." It was exciting, but in a way sad, because with the feelings she'd been harboring for him, the only thing he'd been harboring for her was the desire for her to adopt Molly. Foolish in love, once again.

"And she can't wait to see you, to talk to you, to play with you."

"The way she can't wait to see you, to talk to you, to play with *you*."

"What's this about?" he asked.

"It's about adopting Molly. That's all." About giving Rafe one last chance, about showing Rafe what he was going to be missing. About trying, one last time, to do what she'd promised Grace she'd do. She *had* to do it. Never giving up was also a big part of who she was.

"But I get the impression you're still trying to convince me I should be the one."

"You should, and…" She placed her hand on his chest, her palm pressed flat to his heart. For an instant she felt a little jolt. Felt it so much she nearly pulled back. But it had to be static shock, that was all. "And if you'll let yourself, you'll feel it in here, Rafe. You *are* Molly's father, meant to be. I know it. Grace knew it. Molly knows it."

He pulled back. Stopped for a moment, and simply stared at her. Stared hard, stared deep, then spun and walked away.

Suddenly, the whole idea of adopting Molly scared Edie. What was she thinking? That somehow the three of them could turn into some kind of real family? She loved Molly, she also knew Rafe did. Molly loved both of them back. But the rest of the dots didn't connect, and Edie startlingly realized what she was afraid that Rafe was feeling—that this was a trap meant to either stall the inevitable adoption so she'd have more time to convince him, or to slowly pull Rafe into a place he clearly didn't want to be.

She should have thought it through more carefully. Truthfully, all she'd thought about was Molly. "It's not what you think, Rafe," she called as he headed to the front door. "I'm not trying to back you into a corner here. I only want what's best for Molly."

He stopped for a moment, but didn't turn back to face her. "And how many times do I have to tell you, that's *not* me?"

"Because you don't want to?" Edie cried. "Because you really don't want to? Tell me the truth, Rafe. I know we've argued this over and over but tell me the honest truth now, and I won't say another word." She watched him turn toward her, and saw agony written clearly on his face. It was excruciating, it broke her heart. And in that moment she knew for sure that she loved Rafe Corbett more than life itself, no matter how he felt about her. His pain was so acute to her that his suffering was taking root in her very being. But through the pain, she saw the heart of the man she wanted to be with for ever. A good heart. A kind heart. But a troubled heart. "Tell me, Rafe. Please…"

"It's about loving someone. I can't. Can't love them, don't want to be loved back. Sure, I can do the right things for Molly. Outwardly, go through the motions. But she'll know the difference. She'll see that I don't have that real capacity in me to be anything more than an authority figure, and she needs better than that. I needed better than that, and I know what it's like to be raised by someone who can't, or won't, give you what you need. I was. And now I see so many of my father's traits in me. I look in the mirror and see my father's son. I'm *just* like him, Edie. I was abused. In turn, I abused Rick Navarro. I *am* my father's son and there's nothing I can do about it. His heredity beat me." He spoke his words—words filled with the emotion of an anguished man. Then he was gone.

Edie stood alone in the entry hall, not sure what to do next. Run after him? Leave him alone? Give him his space then go to him?

She didn't know, and as she brushed back the tears on her cheeks there was nothing inside her that could reason this through. Nothing at all. So she left. Went home, sank down in her favorite cozy chair, and wished desperately for her mother. Or for Grace. Or for Rafe.

It was a beautiful evening. Clear black sky, millions of stars, the sound of the bullfrog in the distance croaking out some kind of mating call to his lady love. He'd always felt balanced here. Balanced, accepted, safe. Maybe it was the only place he'd every truly felt that balance, and being here again brought so many memories rushing back. Mostly the good ones, though. And there had been some good ones, especially with Jess. Coming here together, camping out, making plans for their future like nothing was wrong in their lives. Yes, some good times, and he missed those. Missed his brother. Missed that youthful optimism that tried so hard to come through even when everything else was going so wrong. "When I was little, I used to think that when I looked out over the bluff, I could see the edge of the world," he said.

"Is that where it is?" Molly asked innocently. "Over there, where you can't see anything else?"

"No, sweetie. The world is infinitely large. You can't see the edge of it." Even though right now it felt like he was about to fall over that edge. He'd done the right thing, though. He was sure of it. Molly would have everything she needed now.

And he would have…nothing more, nothing less than he'd come with.

"But what's on the other side of where you can't see?"

"A world full of possibilities. Things that will make you happy, things that will help you in your life, things you don't even know about that are waiting for you to find them."

"What kind of things, Rafey? Maybe toys and a kitten?"

"Maybe toys and a kitten. Maybe more people to love you, and for you to love."

"And candy?"

Chuckling, he tousled her hair. "And candy." The innocence of a child…it was magical. Molly was magical, and he was already beginning to miss her. But he'd made the decision and there was no turning back. In his heart of hearts he knew Edie was Molly's mother. That was the only consolation in this. Edie was Molly's mother, and he'd seen that so many times over these past few days. Even seen himself in the father spot, too. Except that couldn't work. "And anything else that makes you happy. It's all out there for you, Molly."

"You, too," she stated seriously. "Except the toys. You're too old to play with toys."

This was tougher than he'd expected. When he'd been young, Hideaway Bluff was where he'd come to make things simple in what was, otherwise, a very complicated life. Yet there was nothing simple here tonight. Not for him, certainly not for Molly. "You're right, I'm too old for toys. But I do have equipment."

"What kind of equipment?"

"Medical equipment. The things I use to help make people feel better."

"Then maybe there's medical equipment out there for you, so you can make lots of people feel better." Sitting on a craggy rock shelf, protected from the elements, Molly snuggled into Rafe's side and laid her head against his chest. "Whatever kind you want, Rafey. Like whatever kind of toys I want."

"And candy," he said wistfully, staring into the campfire he'd built. "Look, Molly, there's something I need to tell you." Instinctively, he put his arm around her shoulders. "It's very, very good."

"Aunt Grace is coming home?" she cried. "When? When is she coming?"

Dear God. He hadn't expected this. Not at all. And he didn't know what to do, what to say. Somehow he'd just figured Molly knew. Granted, everybody had pretty much tiptoed around the subject of Grace's death when Molly was around, but he'd truly thought she understood, and that she was simply taking her time to process it in the way a child would.

He needed Edie here. She was the one with all the right words for children. She was the one with the empathy, the one who instinctively knew what to do. And he was the one who didn't have a clue. Not a single, solitary clue. So maybe it was time to douse the fire and head back. Put this off until he could get to Edie.

But Molly wasn't to be put off. "When, Rafey?" she persisted. "I want to tell her all about Ice Cream, and about my new pony, Lucky. She's beautiful, Rafey. Black and white. And Aunt Grace is going to love her. She always says I can't ride by myself until I'm eight, but with Lucky maybe she'll let me ride by myself when I'm six. Do you think she will, Rafey?"

To break a child's heart…this wasn't the reason he'd come here. In his mind, it should have been a very simple thing. Take Molly to the place he most loved in the world, let her share that feeling with him, then tell her about the wonderful new mother she was about to have. It should have been a good evening, but now this. And he couldn't wait for someone else to take care of it. Molly needed honesty, and understanding. *She needed it from him*—the least likely person in the world to do this.

Rafe drew in a shuddering breath, bracing himself. "Molly, we need to talk about Aunt Grace. And you have to listen to me very carefully, because what we have to talk about isn't going to be easy for you."

"Can we have a party for her? She loves parties, and a nice, big party will make it all better for her. We can have cake and ice cream…the *real* ice cream, not the horse. And maybe party hats."

He remembered those parties his aunt used to

have…parties for all occasions. Big ones, little ones, private ones just for Aunt Grace and him. In his aunt's estimation, a party could cure almost anything, and she had been right. Her parties had cured so many ills, wiped out so much cruelty, eased so many pains, all because her parties had been about caring. About nurturing. "I remember the cakes she used to bake for her parties. My favorite was chocolate, with lots of chocolate icing."

"Mine, too," Molly agreed. "And with sprinkles, too."

"Especially with sprinkles." Glancing out over the vast night expanse in front of him, Rafe wished he could be somewhere out there, having a party with his aunt, listening to her tell the little boy in him that things were going to get better. But he couldn't. And it was foolish of him to think things could be different because there'd never been a moment in his life when he hadn't known who he was, and what he was about. Festive little parties hadn't changed that. "Aunt Grace loved baking those cakes, Molly, and she loved having those parties. Do you know some of the other things she loved, too?"

"Her horses. And you and Jess. She always told me how much she loves you and Jess, that you are her two favorite boys in the whole, wide world."

The lump in his throat hardened. "And you, sweetheart. Aunt Grace loved you more than anything in the world. From the day she brought you home to live with her, she loved you so much, and she wanted you to be her little girl, her daughter…"

"But she's too old," Molly chimed in. "I don't think she is, but the people in charge said she is."

"And they were wrong. In Aunt Grace's heart, you *were* her daughter, and she loved you more than anything."

"Will she again, when she comes back?"

Now the heartbreak. Molly's and his. "Her love for you will never change, Molly. In fact, it's bigger now. Bigger than anything you can imagine. For ever. But Aunt Grace can't come back to tell you how much she loves you. Not any more."

This time, Molly was quiet.

"She got very, very sick. Do you remember that?"

Molly nodded, but still didn't speak.

"She wanted to get better so she could come back and take care of you, and the doctors tried very hard to help her, but it was something the doctors couldn't fix, sweetheart. They tried so hard, and Aunt Grace tried so hard, because she missed you so much, but there wasn't anything anybody could do. Do you remember when she had to go to the hospital?"

Molly nodded. "Summer said it was to get her all better. That when Aunt Grace was better, she'd come home again. But she hasn't. Not yet."

Summer Adair, Aunt Grace's private duty nurse. Summer, herself, had a child, and Rafe knew that anything Summer might have said would have been with sensitivity. But it hadn't been Summer's place to explain the situation to Molly, and now he realized no one had ever taken up that responsibility. They'd simply assumed…too much.

"That's what everybody wanted, sweetheart. Everybody wanted Aunt Grace to get better and come home."

"But she couldn't get better?"

The beginning of the realization. The taking away of innocence. It hurt. "No, she couldn't get better." He paused, searching for the right words… words that wouldn't destroy Molly, words she would understand. Words that came so easily to Edie. "The doctors tried everything they knew how to do. Dr. Rick…he's a very good doctor. You know that, don't you?"

Molly nodded, but didn't speak again.

"Dr. Rick did everything a doctor could do to make Aunt Grace get better, but sometimes even doctors can't fix everything. And he was very sad…we were all very sad because we loved Aunt Grace so much. But she couldn't stay here any longer, Molly. It was time for her to…" He choked on the words, as the tears fell silently down his cheeks. "It was time for her to go to a place where she could be well again, and stay that way for ever. But well in a different way. Molly, sweetheart, Aunt Grace died. Do you know what that means?"

Molly was quiet for a long time, trying to process it. He didn't want to interrupt her, but he also didn't want her to be lost in a dark lonely place. Not the way he'd been for most of his life.

"It means you go to live in heaven," Molly finally said.

"It means Aunt Grace went to live in heaven."

"But I don't want her to go, Rafey! I don't want her to go!" Molly threw herself into Rafe's arms and sobbed…the great, racking sobs of a broken heart, of a child who truly did understand but whose heart was breaking anyway.

"It's OK," he said, holding on to her, rocking her, feeling her tears soaking through his shirt. Feeling his own tears spilling freely down his face. "It's OK, Molly," he soothed, over and over. For Molly, for himself. "Everything's going to be OK."

He said the words, but he didn't know how to make it OK for her. Dear God, he didn't know how. And tonight he ached for Molly the way he'd never ached for anyone else.

"Can I go to heaven, too?" she finally whispered in a tiny, broken voice.

"No, sweetheart. Aunt Grace loved you so much she wanted you to stay here and have the best life you could possibly have."

"But I miss her, Rafey. I want to see her again."

"We all do, Molly." He took a deep breath, sniffed, tried to brace himself…against what, he didn't know. But none of it worked. Right now the world was made up of just the two of them… two broken hearts who could do nothing but sit and hold on to each other. Clinging for dear life. It didn't seem enough, not for him but especially not for Molly. Yet maybe, in the grand scheme of things, this was all there was. "And we'll never stop loving her. But it's in a different way now. It's in here." He placed his hand on her heart, and took her tiny hand and placed it on his. "This is where Aunt Grace is now. She's in our hearts, in a very special place."

Molly thought about that then pulled herself out of Rafe's arms and pointed to the vast openness that extended farther than any eye could see. "She's out there too, Rafey. Where you can't see. You said that's where things will make you happy, where things will help you. And that's where Aunt Grace is."

"In a world full of possibilities," he whispered, gathering Molly back into his arms. "You're right, Molly. That's where Aunt Grace is."

CHAPTER NINE

"No, it's already scheduled. I've got my plane ticket and I'm going home the day after tomorrow. Henry will have all the legalities worked out by then, you can move into Gracie House any time you want, and life will go on."

"So that's it? I sign the papers, you hand Molly over to me, then you leave?" She had known this was what was going to happen, but she hadn't let herself believe it, or even think about it. On one hand, adopting Molly was the best thing she'd ever done in her life but, on the other hand, it was also the most difficult, because it felt like she was shutting all those doors she'd truly believed would open. She'd hoped for a miracle and while she had gotten one, it hadn't been the one she'd planned on, and Rafe wasn't shifting on this whole Molly situation. He was going ahead full steam with his plan, and she couldn't stop him.

"You're not your father," she said. She knew

it with all her heart, but Rafe didn't, and there really wasn't a way to convince him. If his heart wouldn't budge, there was nothing she could do.

"Look what I did to Rick, and he's still pretty scarred from it. That's the way my father acted."

"But you were a boy, Rafe. A boy who was in horrible pain, lashing out. You were thinking with an adolescent's mind, reacting the way an adolescent would. You're a man now. A gentle, compassionate man who takes care of people. What, in there, makes you think you can't love Molly the way she deserves to be loved? The capacity to love isn't dictated by heredity, as you seem to think it is. It's dictated by your heart, and you have a good heart, Rafe. Good, but very scarred."

"In an ideal world, I'd have moved home to Lilly Lake, married you, adopted Molly, practiced at the hospital. But I've never lived in an ideal world, Edie."

"Married me?" she asked. "How can you throw that out there now, when you're two steps shy of stepping on the plane and leaving for ever?"

"I can throw it out there because that would have been my ideal world. We would have dated for a while, the two of us. And the *three* of us would have spent time together, growing as a family. Then…" He shrugged. "Then you would have suffocated. One day you would have woken up and realized I wasn't enough. That maybe I was too emotionally distanced. Or I simply wasn't the kind of support you need. Then where would that leave us? And where would it leave Molly?"

"So, you've got this little life scenario all planned out for us without even including me? How could you do that, Rafe? How could you *assume* us all the way from beginning to end?" They were sitting on the front porch, Edie in the wicker chair, Rafe on the swing. Almost at opposite sides, the way they'd been for days, during the adoption preparations. During those days she'd had the impression, more than once, that Rafe had been on the verge of regretting his decision. Now she knew it. This was what he wanted, but his scars were too tough, his walls too high.

"Just being practical. People don't do that enough. They don't lead with their heads…"

"Because leading with their hearts is so much nicer, Rafe. It takes you to better places, places your head would never allow you." Instinctively, she pushed herself out of the chair then crossed the porch and sat down next to him on the swing. "Your head kept you here, on the opposite side of the porch from me. But my heart put me here, next to you."

"It's not going to work, Edie."

"Why?"

"Maybe that's the question I should be asking you. Why are you fighting so hard for me?"

"Because you're not fighting for yourself."

"I don't need to fight for me. I have a good life, successful career, nice condo…"

"With a porch swing?"

"No!" he snapped. "Just stop it, OK?"

She was getting to him. She knew it, could feel it. So could he, but the feeling was so foreign to him he didn't know what it was. Or maybe loving someone opened you up to the fear of losing them…a fear she knew so well.

"Rafe, when I was a girl, I didn't have a life like all my friends did. My mother was sick, and she truly couldn't get along without me. I took care of her, spent practically all of my childhood taking care of her, and it's what I wanted to do because I loved her. But I lived with this horrible fear…actually, two horrible fears. The first was her death. The doctors were amazed she lived as long as she did, but I think it was because she didn't want to leave me. The second fear was that I would be taken away from my mother. The social workers tried so many times to do that. They thought I needed another life, needed another family…the way you think Molly needs another family. But all I needed was my mother, and everything she was, no matter how hard it got for us sometimes. Consequently I spent a lot of time scared to death they would come and take me away from the person I loved most in the world.

"All those years, that fear never went away. It was with me, day in and day out. And there were a couple of times when they did pull me out of the house and put me in a group home because it was in my own best interests. I know, Rafe, what it feels like to be wrenched out of your life and not be able to do a darned thing about it. But I always ran away, always ran back to my mother because she needed me. More than that, I needed her. Even in her sickest moments I needed her in ways no one could understand. I loved her, Rafe, the way Molly loves you. That's all there was to it. In spite of all the complications and hardships… and there were many hardships…I loved her. It was a simple thing, and nothing else mattered.

"But that love always had this overwhelming dread attached to it because I knew her time was limited, and because I knew I could be taken away from her. So I do know what it's like to have that fear surrounding something you love…*the way you do.* But I also know what it's like to simply let the love happen, no matter what else is going on."

"Then you have a bigger heart than I do," he said, his voice filled with sadness.

"Not bigger. Just one that's found out how to stay open." She twisted to face him and laid her hand on his heart. "Molly could do that for you, if you let her."

"Molly shouldn't have to suffer for my trials and errors." He laid his hand on hers. "Neither should you."

"So you get to make the decision for all three of us? Molly and I don't have a say?"

He pulled her hand to his lips and kissed it. "You see things in me that aren't there. I'm not sure why, but I thank you for it. It makes me feel like I *could* have what you offer…someday. But not now. It's too risky…for you. I'm too risky."

For Rafe, risky translated into not worth loving. She understood that, and it hurt her deeply. Here she was, in love with the man and ready to throw aside all her caution about not getting involved again or waiting until she had more life experience under her belt. All because she'd found the person worth changing for. And she was pretty sure now he loved her back, or else he wouldn't have so much conflict in himself. But maybe the problem here was that *she* wasn't enough. Maybe she'd been deluding herself into believing that all he had to do was believe and they'd have their happily-ever-after when she was the one who didn't have everything Rafe needed to make it come true for himself.

She'd always believed that love was enough, but this time she could have been wrong. Maybe it was time to count her blessings about having Molly in her life, and move on from there. "Life is about taking chances," Edie said, as the sad realization washed down over her. "Everything we do is about taking a chance. Sometimes it works out, sometimes it doesn't. You're not like your father, but you're going to have to put yourself out there in ways that scare you to find out. I hope, someday, that happens for you." With that, she stood and headed to her car, leaving little pieces of her heart behind her. The fight was over. They'd been going round and round for days now, and ending up in the same place they'd started. Now it was time to move past it, time to look forward.

But it was tough to do when so much of what she wanted was behind her.

"I've never pretended differently, Edie. You know that," he called after her.

"Yes, I do know that," she whispered, but not for him to hear as she fought not to cry. This was what she should have expected after all. Rafe wanted a parent for Molly, and he'd got one. No regrets there. Maybe she should chalk it up to another reason to stay out of relationships and get on with it. If nothing else, it sure proved that she didn't know how to pick them. In fact, she was abysmally bad at it. It was so hard, though, because she'd pinned so many hopes on Rafe. And had trusted him to come round. Except she hadn't been enough to make him come round, and that was something she couldn't overcome. She wasn't enough for Rafe, wasn't who Rafe needed.

Well, the bright side was she had a wonderful daughter now, and that did make up for everything else.

As Edie climbed into her car, she fought the urge to look back at Rafe. What was the point? He was done here in Lilly Lake now, and he'd never come back. And she was only beginning here. That was all there was, all there could ever be.

Yet, she did glance back anyway and he was… slumped against the white support column at the top of the steps, leaning there, his head hanging down. He looked like a very sad man, a broken man, actually. But he'd made the choice that had caused that, and there was nothing she could do about it. Yet, in spite of everything, her heart ached for Rafe because he knew what he was losing. Because, like her, his heart was breaking, too.

* * *

"Want to go for a ride?" Rafe called through the bedroom door. He felt like hell, and he didn't want to stay in this house. He needed to get away, spend some last quality time with Molly and make sure she understood what was happening. When he and Edie had told Molly that Edie was going to become her real mother, Molly had been excited. But she hadn't understood why he wasn't going to be part of that family. They'd explained that he had to return to his real home, and Molly seemed to accept it. But who knew? Maybe she was still trying to process it. Or, in her young mind, ignoring it and focusing only on what she wanted. Whatever the case, he needed to spend some time with her. "Molly, did you hear me? Do you want to go for a ride?"

She didn't answer. He didn't blame her.

"We can saddle up Lucky, and you can ride by yourself for a little while." That was something he really did want to do for her before he left here—give her the thrill of riding solo on her very own horse. Or in this case pony. "You can use that saddle Aunt Grace had made for you. Molly?" He knocked again then pressed his ear to the door to listen. But he heard nothing. Not a sound.

"Molly," he said, twisting the knob and pushing the door open a crack. "Are you in there?" A chill of dread was creeping slowly up his spine. "Molly?" he said again, shoving the door all the way back, only to discover what he was afraid he'd discover. She was gone!

"Molly!" he shouted in a voice that resonated throughout the entire house. "Molly, where are you?"

She'd been there half an hour ago. He'd seen her go to her room, seen her start to line up all her dolls for a tea party. "Molly!" he shouted, over and over, as he ran up and down the second-floor hall, opening all the doors and looking in. To no avail. His downstairs search was just as fruitless. So he went to the stable, saw Johnny hand-feeding a new quarter horse arrival that was so emaciated it turned his stomach. Molly had to have known about this horse and she was down here somewhere, helping. That was it. She loved the horses as much as Aunt Grace had, and she was helping with this one.

"I need to talk to Molly," he told Johnny, as he caught a calming breath. "Is she in one of the stalls?"

"Haven't seen her all morning, Rafe. I was surprised that she didn't come down to help me with this beauty..." He stroked the horse's muzzle. "But with her big day coming up, I figured she was busy doing something else."

The words sank in, but slowly. "So what you're telling me is that she isn't here?"

Johnny shook his head. "Haven't seen her since you brought her down last night to say goodnight to Lucky and Ice Cream. Why? Is she missing?"

Panic started rising in him again. "Don't know yet. I thought she was in the house, but she's not. I'd assumed she'd be here."

"Maybe she is, and I haven't seen her," Johnny said. "I've been pretty busy with this one, trying to get her back on her feed. Have you looked around the paddock? Or maybe out in the other stable? I've got a couple of volunteers out there right now, working with some of our problem horses, so maybe Molly's gone out there to help feed or brush them."

"Without permission?"

Johnny shrugged. "Kids are kids. When mine were little, there was always this test of wills going on. Most of the time they did what they were supposed to, but sometimes they did what they wanted to do, no matter what. Molly's a good kid, and smart. When you catch up to her, don't be too hard on her."

"Like my old man would have been?" Rafe snapped, on his way out the rear door. "You were here in those days, so is that what you're telling me? Not to be like my old man was?"

"What I'm telling you is not to be like *any* child's old man who's in a panic over not being able to find his kid," Johnny shot back. "Parents have a way of overreacting when they're scared for their child. I know I did that on more than one occasion. But that's not about your father. It's about you. Be who you are."

Rafe heard the words, heard Johnny call him Molly's parent, and thought about them as he ran to the second stable, only to discover that no one there had seen Molly that day. "Where's her pony?" he asked one of the volunteers who came there as part of the Gracie Foundation.

"In the paddock," a fresh-faced, college-aged volunteer by the name of Ben responded. "We took her out there earlier, along with Ice Cream and a couple of the others. Thought we'd take them over to the pasture later."

But he'd gone by the paddock and hadn't noticed Lucky. Or maybe he hadn't looked thoroughly enough. So on his way back over to the main stable he took another look and Lucky was definitely not there. And Molly's saddle was not hanging in the tack room when he went to find it. "Johnny!" Rafe shouted, on his way back through thc building. "Tell me you did something with Molly's saddle, that you hung it somewhere else. And that Lucky is already down at the pasture to graze."

Johnny's weather-beaten face drained of all color. "I can't, which means I think we have a problem here, Rafe," he said.

Rafe swallowed hard. "Can you saddle Donder for me while I go and make a couple of phone calls?"

"Consider it done," Johnny said. "And I'll be

riding out with you too, Rafe. I feel terrible about this. I knew she wanted to go solo. She's been begging for days. I should have…"

Rafe squeezed the man's shoulder. "Not your fault. Nothing here's been normal for Molly for a while, and I'm hoping she just needed to get away, go someplace to think." Adult reasoning, he knew. But the alternative was that she'd run away, and he didn't even want to think about that. "Give me ten minutes, then I'll be back to ride."

His first call was to Edie. "You haven't seen Molly along the road somewhere, have you?" Stupid question. If Edie had seen her, she'd have stopped.

"Is she missing?" Edie choked.

"Looks like she might have gone for a ride on her pony. We're getting ready to go out looking right now."

"I'm not home yet. I'll turn round and be back in a few minutes."

That's what he'd counted on, what he needed. "I'm going to give Rick a call, in case Molly turns up at the hospital." He did that. "She's missing, Rick," he explained. "Took her pony and left here.

I was hoping she might show up there as the hospital is one of the places where she feels safe."

"I'll alert the staff to be on the lookout. And, Rafe, you shouldn't be going through this alone. I'll be there in a couple minutes to ride out with you."

"I'd appreciate that, Rick," he said, as a knot formed in his throat. "I'd really appreciate that." After all these years Rick had found it in himself to become a friend. It touched Rafe in ways he'd never expected.

"I've looked everywhere, and she's not in the house," Edie called out to the group assembling near the stable door. Johnny was ready to ride, along with his small group of volunteers. And Rafe and Rick were ready to go, both of them looking downright handsome in the saddle, she noticed. In fact, the two of them, together, were breathtaking. She was glad, at least for now, that they were able to work together. "Is Ice Cream saddled for me?"

"You don't have to ride out with us," Rafe called back.

"She's my daughter, Rafe. What else am I supposed to be doing?"

"I'll stay here, in case she comes back," Summer volunteered. "She trusts me, so we should be fine. I'll make some phone calls, and I'll call you if I hear anything from anybody." Summer approached Edie and pulled her into a hug. "I know we've never really spent any time together, but I'm glad you're going to be adopting Molly. Grace thought the world of you, and she'd be happy. And Molly's going to be fine out there. She's a smart, tough little girl. She'll know how to take care of herself."

"I haven't even signed the papers yet, and I'm feeling so…so…"

"So like a mother?" Summer laughed. "Welcome to a mother's world, Edie. It's a great place to live, and it can be more scary than anything you could ever imagine."

Edie climbed up on Ice Cream, patted the horse on the neck then looked down. "And to think that only a few days ago this was one of my biggest fears in the world."

"Grace taught her well, Edie. Trust that."

Summer stepped back then waved her off, while Edie turned Ice Cream in the direction of Rafe and Rick and looked up the hill at the house. Her house, to share with her daughter now. Life had changed so much, so quickly, her head was spinning. But her heart was breaking too, in more pieces than she'd ever known it could, and for the first time in her life she truly understood what her mother had felt all those times the authorities had threatened to remove her from the house, to give her to other people. There was no way to describe the anguish, no way to bear the shattered heart. To love a child…that was all there was, and she felt her mother there with her, guiding her through this ordeal. Felt her mother's strength and courage. That was what sent her to Rafe and Rick and allowed her to ride as hard as they did through the meadow and the hilly incline to the place where Rafe hoped Molly had gone.

"I told her that Aunt Grace was out there," he said, as they paused once to look for any visible signs that Molly had come in this direction. "That somewhere in the distance she could find all her possibilities."

Edie reached over and took hold of his hand. "That was a beautiful thing to say to her."

"But she's not old enough to come up here. It's too dangerous." He gazed up the side of the bluff. "Not steep, but if she doesn't know the way…"

"Nothing over here," Rick called from the far side of a copse of sugar maples. "No sign of a horse or Molly."

"I think I'm going all the way up, and you and Rick can continue around the base and see if you can find anything over there." He started to turn away, but Edie pulled Ice Cream in front of him.

"Rick's fine on his own. I'm going up with you."

Rafe shook his head. "It's too dangerous."

"Yet you took Molly up there?"

"With me. I took her up with me. On the back of my horse."

"But that's the best vantage point up there, isn't it?"

"Best one of the valley, and you can see at least half of the entire estate from there."

"Then I'm going. And you're not stopping me, Rafe."

He reared up in his seat and flagged Rick off in

the other direction, then settled back down. "No, I guess I'm not stopping you, am I?"

"Look, this isn't your fault. I know you're blaming yourself, but—"

"You don't know half of what I'm thinking," he growled, nudging Donder around to head in the direction of the trail leading up, "so just follow me. OK? Keep a couple of lengths back, and you'll be fine."

"But will you?" she asked.

He twisted back in his saddle to look at her. "Do you ever give up?"

"Do you ever give in?"

Rather than answering, Rafe straightened in his seat and urged Donder forward. She knew Rafe was worried. More like scared to death. Blaming himself, too. She knew, because she was going through the same gamut of raw emotions. But at the end of this ordeal she'd have Molly, and Rafe would have… "I guess I don't ever give up," she said, pulling Ice Cream in behind Donder. Because she loved Rafe. When it was all said and done, she loved that stubborn man like crazy, and she wasn't going to give up on him. Not any time soon.

The ride up to the bluff wasn't as difficult as she'd expected, but once at the top her legs felt rubbery and her back was beginning to ache, so she was happy to slip out of the saddle while Rafe had a look around. "It's beautiful up here," she said, gazing out over the great expanse of land.

"Jess and I used to come up here when things got too intense at home. It always felt safe. Probably because I knew the old man was too drunk to come this far looking for me."

"Would he have seen beauty up here if he'd been able to get here?"

"What a joke! Lawrence Corbett see beauty anywhere? Not a chance in hell." He stepped up to the precipice outside the shelf where he and Molly had spent that evening, visored his eyes with his hand, then looked out over the valley below. "He was a miserable man, Edie. Rotten soul. Nothing fazed him, nothing touched him except the ugliness he chose to have around him."

"Yet he was a good doctor?"

"A brilliant doctor, technically. Don't know how

he related to his patients, but no one ever complained, as far as I knew. So I guess he knew how to curb the demon when he was on the job."

"He must have been a miserable man."

"That much is true. He was."

"I mean miserable in his own skin. How could anyone live with himself, straddling the line the way he did? Good doctor, bad person?"

"Guess I've never asked myself that question." He walked over to Donder and pulled a pair of binoculars from his saddle bag. "Probably because I never gave a damn about anything having to do with my old man."

"So why not let him go now, Rafe?" She picked up a fist-sized stone and handed it to him. "This is your father. Throw him over the cliff and be done with him once and for all."

He studied the rock for a moment then tossed it on the ground. "I like the way you care, Edie. Shows me there's still good in the world. But it's not as simple as that. I can't simply hurl everything over the side of the cliff and put an end to the past thirty-five years of my life." He reached out and brushed his thumb across her cheek. "If it were that easy, I'd throw every loose rock up here over the edge. But that's not going to get rid of the one glaringly obvious problem—I am my father's son. I look like him and I act like him."

She took the binoculars and headed back to the edge of the overlook then began to scan below for any signs of Molly or her horse. "Personally, I like the look. At least he left you something good. But as far as acting like him…" She turned herself to face south, and continued looking. "Answer me this one question, Rafe, and answer it honestly. If you weren't afraid that you were like your father, would you keep Molly?" She knew the answer could break her heart, especially if it didn't include her, but she also knew it could be the best thing for Molly.

"Yes," he whispered. "I would."

A single tear clipped down her cheek. "Then you have to keep her. Because here's the thing…" She turned to face west. "Your father wouldn't have come up here looking for Molly this way. His heart wouldn't be ripping in two, thinking about the little girl being out here somewhere, lost. He wouldn't be putting Molly's needs before his own. You are not your father, Rafe. But you are Molly's father, the man who loves her and who would give his own life to protect her. And you would, wouldn't you? You would give up your very life right now if that's what you had to do to save Molly, because you love her more than you love yourself."

"Yes," he choked.

"Then it's settled. I'm not sure how we're going to work out the rest of the details, but for now we don't have to. All we have to do is find Molly." She swiped back her tears then turned to him. "Grace will be happy, Rafe." She'd done her job. Done the right thing. But the pain was unbearable as she didn't know if she would be included in what she'd just done. Rafe had overcome such a major hurdle in his life, but could he overcome another one? Or would it even be fair expecting him to, considering how difficult it had been to get him to realize his feelings for Molly?

Maybe that was as far as it could go.

Before Rafe could respond, his cell phone rang. "That was Rick," he said a moment later. "He said he hasn't found a single clue that would indicate

Molly has even come out this far, so he's going to head out to Jess's cabin, regroup and get ready for a night ride. I think we should do the same thing. Meet Rick at the cabin and regroup."

She glanced up at the setting sun, the gold and pinks of the evening sky, and nodded. "Maybe we'll see something on the way there." She could only hope because even though Molly wasn't going to be her daughter now, that didn't mean the connection was automatically broken. She still felt so linked to that child, still loved her in ways she'd never believed she could love anyone. "I don't want to leave her out there in the dark, alone, all night."

"Neither do I," he said, stepping up to Edie and pulling her into his arms. "But I want you safe in the cabin while I go back out, because I'm not going to put you at risk the way Molly is."

"I can hunt along with you all night, Rafe."

"Maybe *you* can, but I can't do it. The two people I…I love most in the world…I can't have them both at risk."

She heard the words, and they scared her to death, because she truly did want to believe them.

Part of her, though, chalked them up to some kind of emotional reaction to Molly being missing, while part of her hung on to them for dear life. She didn't know what to do, couldn't figure it out right now. Maybe she was afraid to figure it out. So instead of over-thinking the moment, she simply sighed contentedly and stayed in his embrace for another moment. Then she gathered the resolve to push herself away from him. "How about I lead the way back down, and you can bring up the rear? That'll give you a better vantage point in case we've missed something on the way up." Oh, she knew what she'd missed on the way up. And now she was scared to death that she could lose it on the way down. Or lose it after Molly was discovered safe and sound. Or after Rafe came to his senses and remembered what he'd said in the heat of the moment.

But it was all good, she kept telling herself. She'd done what she was supposed to, what she'd promised she would, and the rest of it…well, the only thing she knew for sure was that she loved Rafe, loved Molly. For now, it was enough.

* * *

"At least eat something before you two go out again," Edie insisted, as she scanned Jess's cabinets for anything she could heat up. "Here…some soup. Will you have some soup?" She eyed the propane stove, not sure how to get it going. The cabin wasn't wired for electricity, but Rick had laid a nice fire in the fireplace, so that was good. She wouldn't have to sit alone in the dark once they went back out. And there *was* indoor plumbing.

"You heat the soup," Rick said. "While you're doing that, I'm going to step outside and call my son. Say goodnight, maybe tell him a bedtime story."

What she wanted to be doing with Molly right now. What Rafe *would* be doing with Molly very soon. Or maybe what they'd be doing together.

"And I'm going to look around the cabin to see what Jess left behind in the way of flashlights and batteries. This could turn into a long night." He glanced at Edie. "And soup will be fine. Thank you."

"I'm going to fix a flask of it to take along, in

case you find Molly. She'll need something to warm her up."

"You're going to make a wonderful mother," he said.

"Someday, maybe."

"She's your daughter, Edie. You can't deny that."

"And she's your daughter, too. *You* can't deny that."

For the first time in what seemed like for ever, he managed a smile. "You know I'm a work in progress, don't you? With a lot of emphasis on the work."

"Aren't we all?" she whispered, as she opened the first can and dumped it into a pot. And for the first time her optimism didn't outweigh her fears. It's what she wanted, of course, but now that she was so close to having it all, she was also so close to losing it all. But that was her fear to overcome, wasn't it? The one fear she'd never been able to get rid of.

A loud slam at the front door startled her out of her thoughts, and she looked up to see another large man step inside. One she vaguely recognized, but wasn't sure about.

"Where's Rafe?" he asked.

It had to be Jess. Same voice. Same eyes. "He's in the back room, looking for flashlights."

"And you're...Edie? I think I've seen you around."

"I'm Edie."

He studied her for a moment then smiled. "I always wondered what you'd look like."

"What do you mean?" she asked.

"The woman who could bewitch my brother. Wasn't ever sure it would happen, but I always wondered what she'd look like if someone did. Welcome to the family, such as it is, Edie."

"That's a little premature," she said.

Jess grinned. "I doubt it, but we'll see."

"What the hell are you doing here?" Rafe boomed from the doorway to the back room before Edie had a chance to respond to Jess.

"I came as fast as I could. Caught a helicopter up when I heard what was going on."

"Who called you?" Rafe asked.

"Wasn't you, big brother. It was Rick. Should have been you, but we'll take that up later on. In the meantime, are you up to some night riding?"

"Nothing could stop me, but, Jess, Rick's out there, getting ready to ride, too. He's been solid in this…in everything."

"I can deal with Rick." Jess stepped over to Edie and pulled her into his arms. But briefly. Then he stepped away. "My brother is certainly one lucky son of a…" He cracked a grin at Rafe. "Give me ten to get ready then we're out of here. But just for a couple of hours, if we want to be fresh for morning. And, Edie, if you could open up another can of soup, I'd appreciate it."

She watched the three men eat, and it struck her that they were all very similar. She couldn't explain how, but later, as they mounted up in the dark and she watched them disappear into the night shadows, she knew, for the first time, that they would find Molly. So much power, she thought. Rafe, Rick, Jess…so much power. When she settled down by the fire to wait, that was the thought she clung to.

"You've been to Hideaway Bluff?" Jess asked, as they headed down the west trail.

"Took a good look around a while ago," Rafe

replied. “I took Molly up there the other night. It’s where I think she finally came to terms with Grace’s death, and I thought sure that’s where I’d find Molly.”

“Maybe she’s still trying to find her way out there,” Rick suggested. “We give Molly a lot of credit for being an amazing child, but she’s only five so maybe that’s where she’s still trying to get to and she just hasn’t made it there yet.”

“Then we should go back there,” Rafe said.

“Rick’s right,” Jess said. “In the city, when we do a search and rescue for a child, we always go to the obvious places first, then keep going back to them. Children are predictable. They want to go to someplace they know, someplace they feel safe…like you and I did when we were kids, Rafe. I’m betting that Molly is trying to get to Hideaway Bluff.”

“Not in the dark,” he gasped, thinking of how dangerous it could be. “She wouldn’t…”

“She would,” Rick assured him. “Christopher finds his refuge in the food pantry at home. It’s large enough that he doesn’t feel closed in and small enough that he feels safe.” He chuckled.

"That, plus he knows where I hide the cookies. But, seriously, Jess is right. Kids need that familiarity. If Molly feels a special connection to this place you call Hideaway Bluff, then the chances are she's still trying to get there."

The three of them rode silently back in the direction of the bluff, relying mainly on the moonlit night and stars to guide them, and with every pounding hoofbeat along the trail Rafe thought about his life, the way it had changed, the way it would change. It scared him, but he was ready to face the fear. But everything still boiled down to some basic questions. Could he live in Lilly Lake again, because it might come down to that? Could he really sit on the front porch of Gracie House, look across the street, and not see his old man there or feel his old man haunting him, trying to get under his skin?

The only answer he could find in himself was Edie. She believed, and because of that, he wanted to believe. No, he wasn't there yet, and it might take him a long time to get to where he believed on his own. But for now, maybe leaning on Edie's belief would be enough. It had to be, because he didn't want to lose her.

Of course, there was another consideration in all this. If he couldn't make it here, could Molly survive Boston? Could Edie? Because they were the most important parts of him now, the two essential parts of his equation. The truth was, he was already thinking of the three of them in terms of a family, which was putting the cart well before the horse because his work in progress really did need a hell of a lot of work. So, borrowing from Edie's optimism, they'd just take it one day at a time, the three of them, and figure it out from there.

"Molly's pony!" Rick called from off to the side, closer to the tree line, interrupting Rafe's thoughts. "It's tied up over here."

Rafe and Jess immediately brought their horses around and stopped short of where Lucky was tied, rather loosely, to a sprawling mulberry bush. "Molly!" Rafe shouted into the night.

He listened, but heard only the sound of crickets.

"So she's on foot," Jess said. "Which means

a couple of us need to be on foot, too." He slid off his horse at the same time Rick did. "I think, Rafe, that you should go on up to the bluff again while Rick and I cover this area down here. I don't think Molly's hurt, but she may be getting scared or a little woozy from dehydration, and she might not respond to us when we call so we're going to have to take it slowly. Look under all the bushes, behind all the logs and trees. But I think that if she did make it to the bluff, you need to ride hard to get up there, because she's got no business in a place like that, all alone, in the middle of the night."

"We used to do it," Rafe reminded him.

"But we had each other. That's the difference, big brother. We had each other."

And they still did, he was only now coming to realize. "Look, I'm sorry I've given you a hard time about becoming a firefighter. When this is over, Jess, we need to—"

"I know," Jess interrupted. "And we will."

"I'm glad you're here, little brother. I needed you." He glanced over at Rick. "And him, too. He's a good guy, Jess. We need to do something about him and the hospital. Make him a partner, at the very least."

"I'm glad I'm here, too. You couldn't have kept me away. And about Rick, we'll work it out. Now, get the hell out of here, OK?"

That was exactly what Rafe did. He rode hard through the darkness for the next half-mile, until he came to the trail leading up to the bluff. "Molly!" he yelled, then listened. Nothing. So he dismounted. Taking a horse up there at this time of the night was crazy. By foot was the only sane way, even if it was going to take an eternity. "Molly!" he called again, as he began his ascent.

Every few feet he called again, facing disappointment and a rising level of fear each time when there was no response. Then finally, when he was in sight of the shelf where he and Jess had spent so many nights, he called out one more time, pretty sure by now that this was futile. "Molly, if you can hear me, sweetheart, please say something." It was a cry of desperation. "Please, Molly…" A plea ripped from his heart. "You're not in trouble. I want to make sure you're safe. So if you can hear me…"

"Rafey…" the tiny voice cried out in the night.

When he heard her voice, Rafe shut his eyes, said a silent prayer of thanks, and brushed the tears from his eyes. "Come to Daddy, sweetheart. Come to Daddy."

"She's sleeping peacefully," Edie whispered, tiptoeing from Molly's bedroom. "Exhausted, and glad to be home."

Rafe was sitting on the hall floor outside Molly's room, his back to the wall. He'd allowed Edie to bathe and dress Molly for bed, but he'd refused to go any further than that. "She said she wanted to talk to Aunt Grace."

"Because we were fighting, Rafe. She heard us, and it scared her because she knew we were fighting about her." Edie slipped down to the floor next to him and leaned her head on his shoulder. "We did that to her, Rafe. We scared her."

"I remember when my dad used to get so mean, and I couldn't get away, so I'd hide under the bed and hope he'd go away. Molly wasn't hiding under the bed but it's the same thing, and I know what it's like to be that scared." He took hold of her hand. "I'm going to stay here, Edie."

"In Lilly Lake?"

"In Gracie House. It's not about me any more. I mean, I'm not over all that mess in my past, but I'm moving forward. More than that, I *want* to move forward, and that's because of you."

"Because of Molly," she corrected.

"I would have never let Molly in if it hadn't been for you. And I never meant to hurt you, Edie. All the things I've said, all the arguments…I'm sorry."

"But I'm not," she said. "Because look what you've got. In the end, that's what got you to where you are now."

"You mean with Molly?"

"Of course I mean with Molly. I've always seen it in you, Rafe. Grace knew it was there, too."

"But you love her as much as I do. I always saw *that* in you."

"Loving someone…it's a gift, Rafe. There are so many people out there who are never lucky enough to find it, so when you do have a chance at it, you've got to grab hold and hang on. That's all I wanted you to do. Grab on to Molly and hang on until you found your way. I never thought I'd be part of that because I didn't trust myself enough to think I could. Even now I wonder if I'm everything you and Molly need…"

"Everything, and more."

"So that's the part of me that's *my* work in progress," she said.

"Something I'm going to love working on."

"It's funny, hearing you say that word."

"Love?" he asked.

"Love," she murmured.

"I think it fits pretty well. But I'm going to need practice."

"I think it fits beautifully, and practice all you want."

He stood, then took hold of her hand and pulled her up off the floor. As they walked together through the house, to check the door locks and turn off the lights, they stopped for a moment at the entry to the den to look at the portrait of Aunt Grace. As always, her watchful eye was on them, but tonight her portrait had taken on a glow that made it seem as if she was smiling. She was, Rafe knew. She absolutely was.

As they headed, hand in hand, up the stairs, Rafe scooped Edie into his arms. “I know what I’d like to start practicing, if you’re interested.”

“I thought you’d never ask.”

EPILOGUE

"It is beautiful," Edie whispered, gazing out at the eternity of stars sprawled against the blackest sky. "Like nothing I've ever seen in my life."

"And full of possibilities," Molly added.

It was a perfect night up on the bluff, and the view stretched for ever, the way he always remembered it doing. It was the first time he'd been here with his family…his wife, his daughter. But it wouldn't be the last. "I think she always knew," Rafe said. "Aunt Grace. I think she always knew this was the way it would turn out for us. You, me, Molly…together as a family."

"Do you really think she chose me for you?" Edie asked, as she toasted a marshmallow over the fire Rafe had built. Rafe was refusing the marshmallows but munching away on chocolate-chip cookies. The best he'd ever had, he'd claimed. Even better than his aunt's, he'd told her. But Edie knew, as well as Grace had known, it was just the same old recipe off the back of the chocolate-chip bag. Love had been, and would always be, the ingredient that made them special.

"I'd be surprised if she didn't. That's the way she was."

"And she *would* have let me ride solo," Molly tossed in, still trying to get her way on the issue.

"You *had* your big adventure, young lady," Edie said. "We know you can ride solo, and you know the deal. You can do it only when one of us is there to supervise you. Your daddy or me. Or your Uncle Jess or Dr. Rick, or Johnny when he has the time. No one else."

In the years to come they were going to have their hands full with Molly because she was a strong-willed little girl. Full of life, full of adventure, ready to grab life in a big way. She was like Grace in many ways. Aunt Grace's daughter in every sense of the word. And their daughter too, for which he and Edie said their prayers of thanks every day of their lives.

"Can I have a kitten? And a puppy?"

Rafe slipped his hand into Edie's, and smiled at her. "How about a new horse? We're going out tomorrow to pick up a white stallion, and I have an idea he's going to need lots of attention to make him healthy again. Would that be OK with you? Having a new horse instead?"

"Can I name him Possibility?" Molly asked, looking out into the distance. "Then he'll remind me of where Aunt Grace is."

"I think that would be a very good name for him, honey," Rafe said, sighing the sigh of a contented man.

"A very good name," Edie agreed, handing her daughter the toasted marshmallow. Then she whispered to Rafe, "But we're not letting her name her little sister."

He placed his hand on Edie's belly. It was still their secret, but not for long. "Mary Grace," he whispered back. "For your mother and Aunt Grace."

"Mary Grace," she repeated.

Tonight Mary Parker and Grace Corbett were very happy. Edie felt it, and he felt it too, because he was where he belonged. Rafe Corbet had finally come home. And he'd never, ever leave again. "Mary Grace," he whispered, pulling Edie into his arms.

* * * * *